'You're a bygone species.'

She practically spat the words at him. 'And if you don't turn that wheel and head us back the way we came, I'll see you in gaol for this!'

'Gaol? Don't I get clapped in irons, or strung from the yard-arm? Tame, tame. I'd have thought you could do better than that, Miss Holbrook. I expected a hanging, at least.'

'Don't push your luck, Deveraugh.' Lissa eyed the coil of rope on the guard rail with relish. 'I'd positively enjoy doing the job myself.'

WE HOPE you're enjoying our new addition to our Contemporary Romance series—stories which take a light-hearted look at the Zodiac and show that love can be written in the stars!

Every month you can get to know a different combination of star-crossed lovers, with one story that follows the fortunes of a hero or a heroine when they embark on the romance of a lifetime with somebody born under another sign of the Zodiac. This month features a sizzling love affair between **PISCES** and **SCORPIO**.

To find out more fascinating facts about this month's featured star sign, turn to the back pages of this book. . .

ABOUT THIS MONTH'S AUTHOR

Joanna Neil says: 'With my ruling passion centred on the family and home life, you will guess immediately that I am a Cancerian—a fortunate one, too, in that my husband shares with me the same sign. My practical Capricorn daughter keeps me firmly anchored down to earth, though she constantly amazes me with her creative, artistic talent. My son, an intriguingly perceptive Leo, has a warm, gregarious nature, and is also married to a Cancerian.'

THE WATERS OF EDEN

BY

JOANNA NEIL

MILLS & BOON LIMITED
ETON HOUSE   18–24 PARADISE ROAD
RICHMOND   SURREY   TW9 1SR

First published in Great Britain 1993
by Mills & Boon Limited

© Joanna Neil 1993

Australian copyright 1993
Philippine copyright 1993
This edition 1993

ISBN 0 263 77905 X

STARSIGN ROMANCES is a trademark of Harlequin Enterprises B.V., Fribourg Branch. Mills and Boon is an authorised user.

Set in 10 on 12 pt Linotron Palatino
01-9302-49494 Z

Typeset in Great Britain by Centracet, Cambridge
Made and printed in Great Britain

CHAPTER ONE

LISSA adjusted her foothold on the sloping riverbank and stared crossly at the cabin cruiser moored on the gently rippling water. What was the wretched man doing on board, anyway? Not just on board, but stretched out along the wooden bench, for heaven's sake, as if he hadn't a care in the world, as if he owned the place. It was aggravating in the extreme to discover him there, just when she had hoped to find the launch deserted. How was she ever going to get the chance to think things through if her last sanctuary had been commandeered by an absenting workman?

'Excuse me——' she called. The man gave no indication that he had heard, and she frowned, a small, thin line etching itself into her smooth brow. He belonged to the stunt crew's management team, didn't he? She'd seen him earlier, talking to one of the men setting up the car ramps on the far side of the field. Well, he wasn't exactly the sort of man you could overlook, was he? She surveyed his long-limbed body with an attempt at cool detachment, her gaze flickering over the dark denims that moulded his strong thighs, and the jade sweater that clung to his hard male chest.

Abruptly, she drew in her breath. He'd have to go. She needed to be alone, and there was nowhere among all the tents and sideshows where she could hope to escape the milling crowd. There were enough activities going on around the field; surely there was somewhere his services were needed?

'Excuse me,' she said again, raising her voice a notch. 'Will you come down off there?'

He stirred and stretched lazily, crossing one leg over the other, and proceeded to settle his feet more comfortably on the glossy planking. For all the attention he paid her, she might not have been there.

Lissa's mouth tightened. 'I hope I'm not interrupting anything?' Her tone was drenched in sarcasm.

Moving his head a fraction, he opened his eyes the merest slit and scowled at her from under thick dark lashes. 'You are, as a matter of fact,' he muttered. 'I'm trying to sleep, if you have no objections?'

With an irritating lack of urgency he closed his eyes again and sank back into oblivion, leaving Lissa to grind her teeth in frustration.

A quick survey of the distant marquees did nothing to restore her equilibrium. She recognised the lean figure of Richard Blake moving towards the exhibition stand, and the last thing she wanted right now was for him to notice her. She had far too much on her mind to take time out to deal with him. In fact, it could well be that his knowledge of her return to Eastlake had brought about her present anxieties. The whole matter needed a lot of thought. At least she could try to snatch an hour or so's grace.

Putting a clamp on her growing exasperation, she returned to her contemplation of the recumbent form on the bench. Obviously, she was disturbing him, but she refused to acknowledge the twinge of guilt that prodded her. He was being paid to work, wasn't he, not to lie down on the job?

Coolly, she said, 'I'm sorry if I'm bothering you, but I really would like to come on board. Would you open up the rail gate?'

At her words, his knees twitched, a muscle jerked in the shadowed plane of his cheek. At last she seemed to be getting through to him. Slowly, he swung his feet down to the floor and sat up, experimentally flexing a pair of broad shoulders to ease an apparent tension. Early thirties, she decided, studying him thoughtfully. He blinked, glanced her way, and then blinked again, his eyes sharpening into sudden focus. This time, when his glance slid over her, his scrutiny was compounded of interest and a totally male appreciation. It was a look she was used to, and she ignored it.

'I was surprised to find anyone on board,' she told him. 'Shouldn't you be with the rest of your team?'

'My team?' he said on a note of query, his dark brow lifting negligently.

She bit down on her impatience. He was miles away, his brain fogged with sleep. 'The last I saw of them, they were all busy checking the distances for the car jump,' she said. 'Oughtn't you to be with them?'

'Ah——' He examined his footwear thoughtfully for a moment. 'But you know,' he murmured, 'there were things to be done on the boat. It will be needed later on.'

He would say that wouldn't he? He had to account for his presence on the cruiser, after all.

'I realise that,' she said. 'But that's another hour away yet. I'd like a short time on board before the start, if you wouldn't mind.'

It was all the same if he did. This morning's episode at the flat had shaken her up quite a bit, and she needed desperately to have some time to herself in quiet surroundings. The crowded fête with all the people thronging around provided no privacy. This was the only place she could think of.

He stood up and walked across the deck to stand by the chromium guard rail, looking down at her. Lissa moved restively. His appearance was profoundly unsettling. Apart from the inordinate length of those legs, and the firm muscularity of his biceps evident beneath the dark sweater, there was something about the thrust of that strong male jaw that invited a second look. His eyes, too, were strangely compelling, startlingly blue.

With an effort, she pulled herself together. Her rickety composure had nothing whatever to do with him. It was the shock of receiving that envelope and its portentous contents at breakfast-time that was making her feel so edgy. That, and the narrowly missed encounter with Richard Blake after the intervening four years. How could she be expected to remain calm?

'Perhaps you would help me up on deck?' she ventured expectantly, adding with a bewitchingly brief smile, 'I'd hoped to be alone for a while.' After all, if he wasn't going to take a hint, she simply had no choice but to be blunt.

He regarded her steadily. 'I'd rather hoped to enjoy

the same conditions myself.' His voice was deep and attractive, smoothing along her nerve fibres like cool silk, but there was no hint of apology or intent to abdicate his position.

Her chin lifted. Surely her need was greater than his? Out of the corner of her eye, she saw that Richard Blake was on the move again, and inwardly she groaned. She wouldn't let this man sway her from her course.

'Look, Mr——' She threw him an enquiring glance.

'Deveraugh,' he obliged. 'Rourke Deveraugh.'

'Mr Deveraugh, perhaps when you've finished work for the day, you'll be able to find all the peace and seclusion you're looking for. In the meantime, I'd be really grateful if you'd step aside and let me come on board for a while.'

Despite the sunshine, it was a crisp, cold day, and she pulled up the collar of her black jacket, flicking the long auburn mane of her hair out of the way. 'That isn't too much to ask, is it?' The burnished waves rippled and settled, and Deveraugh's glance followed the movement.

His hands gripped the rail firmly. He said, 'It's really a matter of viewpoint. Maybe you're not fully acquainted with my exact role here?'

Her mouth tilted. 'Oh, come on, Deveraugh, quit messing around and let me on the damn boat.'

He shook his head. 'Can't do that, I'm afraid. Security.'

'What?' The word escaped her in a small explosion of sound. 'You're not seriously expecting me to believe that?' It was clearly time to be assertive. 'I'm the one person who can step on board without reprisal. Lissa Holbrook—have you heard the name? I'm going to be floating down river on this thing later this afternoon, so you don't need to have any worries about letting me up on deck.'

He appeared to be thinking it through. 'Identification?'

Her jaw dropped. He was actually persisting with this farce. 'In this outfit?' she said tightly. 'Where would I keep anything, do you imagine?'

His blue gaze slanted over her assessingly. Hip-hugging black jeans tucked into hand-tooled black leather boots, clinging black sweater beneath the open black jacket. It had been the photographer's idea. It made her look dramatic and sexy, he'd said. Good publicity.

Deveraugh grinned, his teeth showing very white, very even. 'No ID,' he drawled, 'no access.'

Her eyes narrowed into a steely glare. 'Oh, wait a minute,' she said furiously, raking through the pockets of her jacket. 'Here, hold these.' She slammed her keys into his hand and he studied the silver tag on the ring with curiosity. The topaz eye of the scorpion glinted up at him.

'Zodiac, huh? Is this supposed to enlighten me?'

Still searching through her pockets, she muttered fiercely, 'My name's engraved on it somewhere; doesn't that fulfil the object of the exercise?'

'Too, small,' he commented. 'You'd need a magnifying glass to make it out properly. Besides, I'd sooner avoid anything that sniffs of the predator.'

Her breath hissed through her teeth. How could

he say that, when he had all the makings of one himself? Her glance seared his hard, angular face. What was he? she wondered. Lion? Ram?

'Beginning of March,' he said drily. 'What does that make me?'

'A pain in the neck,' she retorted, pushing her cash-card towards him. She flicked her head in the direction of the card. 'Does that meet with your approval?'

He looked at the small piece of plastic. 'That'll do nicely, ma'am.'

Lissa thrust her belongings back into her jacket, bending her head to hide from him the secretive smile that touched her lips. Pisces, she thought, her confidence returning. When it came to confrontation, what possible match was a fish for a scorpion?

Straightening, she watched as he undid the holding gate, and then held out a hand towards her. The feel of his strong fingers enclosing her small palm came as something of a shock to her system. His grip was firm, the touch of his forearm supportive at her elbow. It confused her, that contact, and she broke away as soon as she felt the solid deck beneath her feet.

She glanced back at the marquees, but there was no sign of Richard. He had disappeared into the crowd.

'Are you trying to avoid someone?' Rourke asked.

'I'm trying to get a little privacy,' she murmured, going over to the far side of the boat where she would be hidden from view.

'You could try the cabin,' he suggested, and she

thought about it, but only for a moment. Maybe when he had gone—his was a powerful enough presence out here; she didn't care to think what effect the restricting confines of the cabin might have if he should follow her.

'I prefer the fresh air,' she muttered, and coloured faintly as she detected the slight upward twisting of his lips.

Holding her head high, she went over to the rail and rested her fingers on the chrome, looking out over the sparkling, sun-streaked water. She stayed there for a long time.

It should have calmed her, gazing down at the burbling river, should have helped her to think about the problem uppermost in her mind; but it was impossible to concentrate, knowing that he was close by. She heard him moving about, checking things on the boat. Why didn't he take himself off, somewhere else? How could she think straight, with him around? He exuded masculinity in the way that a flame gave out heat.

'You should learn to relax,' he murmured, and she jumped at the sound of his voice right next to her ear. 'See what I mean?' he said softly. 'You're all strung out like a tight wire. What's bothering you? Are you worried about the stunt?'

Was she? Was that what the horoscope was hinting at—that cold, anonymous missive that had been pushed under her door this morning? *A venture you are planning could be fraught with disaster*. Lissa shivered. A warning, or a threat. . .it had sinister overtones. Who could have sent her something like that? Each word was cut out from different magazines and newsprint, and pasted to a square piece of card.

'There's really nothing to be concerned about.' Rourke's words cut across her preoccupation, and she sucked in her breath a little shakily.

'No, of course there isn't,' she agreed, 'It's just a boat ride. All I have to do is position myself against the banner. What could possibly go wrong?' She glanced around the neat deck. 'Everything's been checked over, hasn't it?'

He nodded. 'The motor was running earlier, smooth as honey.'

Lissa accepted the comfort of his assurances. She did not really believe anything untoward was going to happen this afternoon. No, the threat behind the horoscope had been deeper and more insidious than that. *Work and health matters suffer in a return to familiar ground.* What did it mean? That it had been a mistake to come back to Eastlake?

The decision had seemed a natural one at the time. When she had finished her course at the university, the pull of her home town had been a strong one. Even though her parents had moved to the States, she still had friends here, people she had grown up with. Of course, she missed her family, but her father's promotion to foreign correspondent had been too good a chance for him to miss.

Her own future lay in this small town. She had just begun to setttle into her neat flat, and although it wasn't furnished expensively the few pieces she had were chosen with loving care. Adam had been more than helpful, when it came to moving in. She wished that she had been able to spot him in the crowd. Just the presence of a familiar, friendly face might have made her feel better.

One thing was certain, though. She couldn't give in to intimidation. Now she was set to make a go of her programming business, and nothing was going to stop her. Moodily, she scuffed the toe of her boot against the deck rail. She wouldn't allow anyone to drive her away.

'Do you want to talk about it?' Rourke was watching her, and she was disturbed by the uncanny perception lurking in the blue gaze. This man would want to know everything, would delve and dig, and not be satisfied with surface explanations.

Her jaw took on a mutinous slant. 'There's nothing to talk about,' she gritted. It was none of his business, anyway. Why didn't he go away? 'Isn't there some work you should be doing?'

Moving away from him to a place further along the deck, she grimaced at her own rudeness. She was as tense as a cat stalking a bird. Perhaps it was the waiting getting to her. She wasn't used to inactivity, and Deveraugh hadn't helped any by hanging around. In some indefinable way he just added to her restlessness.

Still, she reflected soberly as she stared down at the water, being on the boat had at least served to clarify her thoughts in one direction. There was no sense in letting a silly thing like an unsolicited horoscope put her in a flap. She would not let herself be diverted; she would go on exactly as she had planned.

It might be reassuring, though, to talk things over with Adam, and there would be no better opportunity than this afternoon. A chance, too, perhaps, to sort out the business deal they had talked about last week.

She glanced down at her watch. If Deveraugh was going to persist in trailing her every move, there was no point in staying here. The photographer would be waiting for her by the exhibition stand in twenty minutes or so. Anyway, her short stay on board had at least served some purpose. It had kept her out of Richard's way. With any luck he would have disappeared by now, caught up in discussions with prospective clients, and by the time he found her she would be too involved in other matters to be cornered.

Her eyes scanned the horizon. Adam must be around somewhere—if she could just find him and have a quick word before her part in the proceedings began—— As if in answer to her prayers, a small group of business-suited men began to disperse, and the figure of a fair-haired man came into view. Lissa sighed with relief, his name hovering on her lips, and it was only when Rourke's head turned sharply that she realised she had spoken aloud.

'Have you seen someone you know?' He followed the direction of her gaze and she nodded.

'I think so. Adam Franklyn—his company owns this land and he gave permission for the event to be held here. I've been looking for him all afternoon, but he must have been tied up with work. I must go and see him.'

Rourke's eyes had narrowed, but she dismissed the problem of his reactions from her mind as she moved to the rail gate.

If she was quick, she and Adam could grab a coffee in the refreshments tent and find a moment to talk.

Stepping off the boat, she smiled sweetly at Rourke. 'Thanks for letting me on board,' she said. 'You make a good security guard. Maybe you missed your vocation?'

His mouth made a wry twist. 'Count yourself lucky I didn't frisk you,' he told her, and she eyed him warily as she backed away.

'That's more than you'd dare, Deveraugh,' she threw at him from the relative safety of the riverbank, and he laughed softly, the sound of it filling her ears as she sped across the grass.

Adam turned as she approached. 'Lissa, sweetheart,' he greeted her as she drew close, 'where did you come from? I was looking for you earlier.'

He put an arm round her and hugged her to him in the familiar, easy fashion she was used to. 'I grabbed a few minutes to myself,' she explained breathlessly. 'I couldn't concentrate, with all these people around.'

'I know just what you mean,' he nodded. 'I haven't had a minute to myself since the fête opened. Mind you, it's been good for business, so I suppose I shouldn't complain.' He grinned and she felt her spirits rise as she looked with affection at this man who was like a brother to her.

'Why don't I buy you a coffee?' she suggested, and they began to walk towards the refreshment tent,

Lissa's glance drifting idly back towards the boat.
Rourke stood on the deck, tall, unmoving, his brooding, watchful presence enveloping her as though he
were by her side.

'Hamburgers,' Adam drooled, sampling the air
appreciatively as they stepped under the canvas
awning. 'I haven't had a thing to eat for hours—
since breakfast, anyway.'

'Then hamburgers it shall be,' she laughed, loading
up a tray. 'We can't have you fading away to nothing,
after you've done so well for yourself these last few
years.' Finding an empty table at the far side of the
tent, they sat down and Lissa stirred sugar into her
coffee. 'I never dreamed I'd come back to find you at
the head of a company. You'd better tuck in, stoke
up your energy supplies. Lynx Engineering needs
you.'

'We had a good turn-out today,' Adam said, biting
a huge chunk out of the burger. 'The weather helps,
of course. A nice dry day can do wonders for ticket
sales. I've been dealing with enquiries for our prod-
ucts all day. It'll mean a full order book.'

'I thought you were working flat-out already? Your
poor wife can't be seeing much of you as it is.'

He pulled a face. 'Can't be helped, I'm afraid. We
need to push forward all the time—that's the driving
force behind any kind of business.'

Lissa could sympathise. Wasn't she motivated by
the same inner compulsion, the urge to forge ahead?
Raising her coffee-cup to her lips, she stiffened
suddenly as Rourke came and stood by the entrance
to the tent. He was not alone. His companion, a

pretty, dark-haired woman, was taking up all of his attention, and Lissa frowned over the rim of the cup. He certainly didn't appear to be overburdened with guilt about leaving the rest of his crew to do all the work. It was obviously far more interesting to spend his time chatting up the local talent.

Over Adam's shoulder, she watched as the couple moved to stand together in a quiet corner, deeply engrossed in each other. Lissa's mouth shaped her distaste, and she put her cup down and realised with a start that Adam was saying something.

'This afternoon's coverage should go a long way in helping you set up your own firm,' he said, wiping his hands on a serviette. 'Have you found many openings so far?'

'A few,' she agreed. 'I've made some contacts that I can follow up over the next couple of weeks. Have you thought any more about our contract? I'm sure I can come up with something that would simplify things for you.'

'I have,' he admitted, throwing the used tissue into a nearby bin. 'But we'll need to talk it through, and I can't do that right now. I've a meeting with one of the advertisers in five minutes. What say we get together after your trip down river if you can manage it?'

'That sounds fine.' This wasn't the moment to tell him about her earlier worries. She would mention it some other time.

Adam stood up and gave her another hug. 'See you later, then. Have fun on the boat ride.'

She watched him go, noting at the same time that

Rourke's companion was no longer in evidence. A fact that seemed to have soured him, judging from his grim expression.

'At a loose end, Deveraugh?' she queried disdainfully as he followed her out of the tent.

'You know he's married, don't you?' he asked, his tone brusque.

'Is that significant?'

'It should be. When I saw you with your arms around each other, I thought maybe it needed pointing out.'

Her manner was equally terse. 'You hadn't considered that it had nothing to do with you, I suppose? Your own ethics are totally beyond question?'

'Take my advice and leave well alone. I'd hate to see a marriage broken up.'

'Don't concern yourself,' she said through her teeth. 'I'm sure if he wants your interference he'll ask for it.'

Rourke studied her. 'I guessed something was wrong on the boat, and now I know what it was. You were scratchy as a cat on the prowl. What happened? Did I mess up your plans by being in the wrong place at the wrong time?'

Her green eyes slitted. 'Butt out, Deveraugh. Your opinions aren't needed here. If I want to see Adam Franklyn, I'll do so, with or without your approval. In fact,' she added, driven by an unholy desire to be perverse, 'I shall be meeting him after the boat ride. We'll have more time together then.' Let him pick the bones out of that, she thought with satisfaction, but the look he gave her was oddly enigmatic.

'Is that your last word on the subject?' he asked coolly, and she gave him a wintry smile.

'Definitely. Goodbye, Mr Deveraugh. Don't let me keep you from your work. I'm sure you must have plenty to occupy yourself with. A stray brunette, perhaps?'

With that, she turned and stalked away towards the exhibition stand where the photographer was waiting, camera slung over his shoulder.

It seemed like an eternity before the shots were taken and the interview with the local Press was wrapped up. There would be more photos, but they would be taken as the cruiser pulled away, and she needn't concern herself about those. The sooner it was all over, the better. She hated being the centre of attention, but at least it would serve to stir up an interest in her business. What better way to get it off the ground than by leading an armada of rafts up river, parading before the assembled crowd of onlookers?

By the time she reached the boat once more, the banner had been fixed in place, and all she had to do was position herself against it, her body making the bold black outline of the letter T—Trends was the name of her company—emblazoned across the white silk.

Gripping the leather straps provided, she settled herself against the supporting pole.

'Need any help?' Glinting blue eyes scanned her slender form.

'What are you doing here?' She scowled at Rourke. 'Go away.'

'My, tetchy, aren't we? I was only asking if you wanted any assistance.'

'I want nothing from you,' she said stormily, 'except to see the back of your head.'

'That can be arranged,' he murmured silkily, completely unperturbed by her show of temper. 'Smile nicely for the cameras.' She glared at him as he walked away. Bothersome man.

Even now, he wasn't taking himself off. No, he had to stop and talk to the men checking the steel braces, didn't he? Anything to delay matters and annoy her. Why he needed to choose this moment to pass the time of day with all and sundry and—good grief!—take a wad of notes from his back pocket and count them out with infuriating slowness—was anybody's guess.

She fumed in silence, turning her gaze towards the soothing vista of river and fields, and the brightly coloured assortment of rafts that bobbed gently on the water. He was doing it deliberately, purely to torment her. Well, he was wasting his time. She would look out over the scenery and think serene thoughts, and before too long Rourke Deveraugh would be nothing more than a hazy memory, a burr on the skin that was shaken off and trampled underfoot.

The sound of the engine starting up was a welcome intrusion, the smooth glide of the craft as it moved out into the main stream a gratifying feeling. She closed her eyes, and lifted her face to the sun, enjoying its light, warm caress on her cheeks. A breeze sprang up, playfully teasing the chestnut curls of her hair so that they fluttered and tumbled against the banner. Time spun out in a silken band.

Lazily, she stretched and smiled, letting her somnolent gaze drift over the procession of reeds and gnarled trees that dipped their branches low into the water. Way in the distance was the field where the fête was being held. Gone was the flotilla of rafts that had followed majestically in the wake of the cruiser.

Her eyes snapped open, wide, green and full of a growing suspicion. Gone? Where had they gone? She turned her head to direct her glance over the man at the wheel.

'What exactly do you think you're doing, Deveraugh? This is not the route. Why are you at the wheel?'

'Complaints,' he drawled, without turning around, 'nothing but complaints. I thought you said you wanted to see the back of my head? There's really no pleasing you, is there?'

'Where are we?' she demanded, letting go the supports and marching over to him. 'Why aren't we with the rest of the craft?'

'A slight alteration to the plans,' he murmured. 'I fancied a change of scene. Nothing to worry about.'

'I'm not worried,' she snapped. 'I'm furious. We had a schedule to follow. You can't up and change it just like that.'

He looked surprised. 'Why not?' he asked blandly.

Lissa made a sound that was something between a hiss and a growl. 'Because,' she said fiercely, 'this is the twentieth century—the age of piracy was stamped out aeons ago.'

'What a dismal thought,' he commented soberly. 'Still, we could always revive it, couldn't we?'

CHAPTER TWO

LISSA stared at him, outrage framing her mouth, rendering her momentarily speechless. He was a madman, wasn't he? There was no other explanation; she'd gone and landed herself in the sole company of a madman. Well, whether he was crazy or not, she'd make him rue the day he chose to cross her. Anger rose like a bitter tide in her throat.

'Mr Deveraugh,' she said, shaping the words with lips flattened by barely suppressed rage, 'you will turn this boat around, right now, and head us back in the direction of the rafts.'

He shook his head. 'And waste a lovely, bright afternoon like this, drifting with the crowd? I'm afraid not, Miss Holbrook; that idea doesn't appeal to me at all.'

'I really don't much care,' she snapped, 'about what appeals or does not appeal to that obnoxious mire you call a mind. I demand that you take me back to the others now, this minute.'

'Sorry,' he shrugged with casual negligence, 'but I can't oblige.'

'Can't? *Can't?*' Her palm itched to slap the bland indifference from his face. *'Won't* is more like it. Do you know what you are, Deveraugh? You're a brigand, a throw-back to the Dark Ages. Well, let me tell you,' she flung at him acidly, 'you're a bygone species, you're on your way out, and if you don't turn that wheel and head us back the way we came I'll see you in gaol for this faster than you can say pieces of eight.'

He cast her a sidelong glance. 'Gaol? Don't I get clapped in irons, or strung from the yard-arm? Tame, tame. I'd have thought you could do better than that, Miss Holbrook. I expected a hanging, at least.'

'Don't push your luck, Deveraugh.' She eyed the coil of rope on the guard rail with relish. 'I'd positively enjoy doing the job myself.'

His crooked grin did nothing to calm her blistering temper, neither did his bantering tone. 'Where's your spirit of adventure? Haven't you any taste for travelling into the unknown, giving yourself up to the pull of the elements?'

'With you for company?' Her tone lashed him with scalding contempt. 'A fiend—a by-blow from the devil's spawn?'

She marked with satisfaction that he appeared to brood on that. 'Do you know,' he murmured, 'that thought had never occurred to me? Next time I'm down in Surrey I shall have to have words with my mother. I'd no idea she was such a fast lady. She always led me to believe my father was a solid company man—rose through the ranks to become managing director, or so I understood.' He paused, his eyes narrowed in speculation. 'I wonder if he knows? He always said I had the luck of Lucifer.'

'You have a warped sense of humour,' she informed him coldly. 'I, on the other hand, don't find anything remotely funny in this situation. Hasn't it crossed your mind that we will be missed, the others will be wondering what has happened? If you had any sense at all you would start back now before they come looking for us.'

'They won't, you know,' he stated dismissively. 'They're all far too busy taking part in the competition for the best raft to be interested in what we're doing.'

Smarting, Lissa absorbed the unpalatable truth of that. No one was going to come looking for her. She was on her own.

She cast a murderous look over his hard male profile. OK, so he was well-built, and he was going to make a tough opponent, but there had to be some chink she could work at. It was just a question of finding it.

He said, 'Why don't you relax? Enjoy the day for itself.'

'*Relax*?' she echoed tersely. 'The whole point of this afternoon was to advertise my company, not to go for a jaunt along the river.'

'This way, you get to do both,' he reasoned with galling unconcern. 'And, if you're honest with yourself, you'll remember that earlier today a little peace and quiet was high on your agenda.' His well-shaped mouth curved attractively. 'You and I have something in common, you see.'

'Oh, no,' she said abruptly. 'No way. You and I have nothing in common. Absolutely nothing.'

He contrived to look hurt. 'Aren't you being a little harsh, Lissa? Do you always form opinions straight off the top of your head?' He sent her an enquiring glance.

'Where you're concerned, two seconds would be stretching it. My patience is fast running out, Deveraugh—I've already told you, several times, that I do not wish to go any further along the river. Take me home.'

'All in good time,' he murmured, blithely continuing on course. 'I have it in mind to visit a small lake just around the bend.'

Gripping the rail, she struggled to keep a check on her boiling emotions. Short of battering him on the head with a blunt instrument—the thought held immense appeal, and she savoured it for a long moment, before reluctantly putting it on hold—she couldn't come up with any way out of the present situation. No one was within earshot, they were miles from anywhere, it seemed, and even if she jumped in the river and swam for it the chance that she would outmanoeuvre him in the water was slim. Maybe when they reached the lake some better opportunity would present itself.

'How is it that you managed to get behind the wheel, anyway?' she enquired, her voice curt. 'What have you done with the skipper?' She cast a suspicious glance over the lockers and then shook herself for her wild imaginings.

He chuckled. 'Nothing as drastic as that. He proved to be quite open to my proposition.'

'Proposition?' Then, 'The money,' she said with a snap, as her brain clicked into fourth gear. 'You paid him, didn't you? Bribery and corruption. Just wait till I get my hands on that man.'

'Trouble, huh?' His tongue made a clicking sound, and Lissa glowered at him.

'You needn't be so complacent,' she warned hotly. 'You've a lot to answer for. Not least, the fact that you've deserted your fellow workers. I imagine they didn't even cross your mind?'

He shrugged. 'I've done my bit for the day.'

'You've done more than enough', she retorted. 'Maybe by tomorrow you'll come to realise the folly of your actions, especially if you find you've no job to go back to.'

'You really ought to calm yourself,' he told her mildly. 'You're wasting an awful lot of energy hopping up and down like that.'

'I am not hopping,' she declared angrily, stamping her foot against the planking.

He looked at her doubtfully. 'If you say so.'

She sucked in a deep breath. 'Look, Deveraugh,' she said, 'it isn't too late, even now. If you turn this thing around and take me back, I promise I'll say nothing of what has happened.'

'We're almost at the lake,' he said. 'See? We'll tie up on the island and stretch our legs a bit. You'll feel better then.'

She sent him a dark scowl. The island, a small green tree-covered expanse in the middle of a smooth, glassy lake, came into closer view, and edgily she cast a glance around the boat for some kind of weapon.

He intercepted the look. 'All the hardware's locked away,' he informed her. 'But you won't be needing it.'

'I'm so glad you think so,' she remarked with caustic restraint, 'but if I were you I wouldn't turn my back.'

'Is violence a trait of yours?'

'I'm not used to being abducted,' she said, tight-lipped. 'I'd like to know why you've brought me here.'

'Of course,' he agreed. 'You'll find out soon enough. But for the moment let's concentrate on getting the boat moored, and ourselves on to dry land.'

Her hopes that he might leave something to chance and throw her the opportunity to make her own way back faded as she saw him lock up and pocket the key. She would have to think again.

'I'm not good at waiting,' she persisted stubbornly, as he handed her down from the cruiser.

His mouth indented. 'You'll learn.' He indicated a rough path that led to a sturdy wooden cabin, and she dug her heels into the ground.

'I am not walking to any hut with you,' she assured him with icy defiance.

'Would you prefer I carry you?' He advanced towards her and she flung him a look full of wrath, annoyingly conscious of his height and the wide breadth of his shoulders.

'Don't you dare,' she snapped. Frustration and smouldering resentment warred inside her. It was unbelievable. How could this be happening to her? This feeling of utter helplessness, of being buffeted by the whims of some other person, was new and decidedly unsettling. It made her want to rant and rave and kick out at something—preferably him.

She viewed the cabin through hostile, narrowed eyes. 'What's in there?'

'Fishing gear, mostly,' he said. 'What did you expect? A double bed and mirrors?'

Colour rode high on her cheekbones. 'Believe me, you'd live to regret it if there was.'

His gaze slanted over her. 'I'll bear that in mind.' She thought she detected the ghost of amusement in his blue eyes and it incensed her even more.

'If it's not completely beyond you,' she said glacially, as they reached the hut, 'perhaps you could tell me why we are checking out fishing equipment?'

'It's the usual practice, if you plan on spending the afternoon fishing.'

'Fishing?' she repeated, astonishment temporarily swamping her anger.

'Well,' he murmured, studying the lock on the cabin door, 'of course you don't have to, if you prefer not.'

Once again, she felt an overwhelming urge to knock a wedge in his complacency. Bide your time, Lissa, she told herself, bide your time.

Her finely shaped brows met in dark disapproval as she watched him pick at the lock with a thin piece of wire that he had produced from somewhere in the depths of his pocket. 'Isn't that against the law?' she prodded stiffly.

'Possibly,' he muttered, frowning. He didn't

bother to lift his eyes from the task in hand. Clearly, the lock was proving difficult.

'Not that abiding by the law would be a matter of supreme importance to you,' she sniffed.

He aimed a hefty kick at the door, and there was a splintering sound as wood gave way to metal. A smile of satisfaction added a roguish slant to his mouth. 'Sorry,' he said, returning his attention to her. 'What were you saying?'

Her teeth met. 'Forget it,' she said.

He pushed open what was left of the door, and went inside the hut. 'Why don't you come on in?' he invited cordially. 'It's quite clean, no spiders or anything. The walls have been painted with a white emulsion. It appears to have put them off.'

Obstinately, she remained outside. 'You can't get away with this sort of thing, you know,' she warned grimly. 'First abduction, now breaking and entering, not to mention the theft of a boat. Your deeds will catch up with you sooner or later, mark my words.'

'As long as it's later,' he remarked with cheerful optimism, 'I'll try not to let it worry me.' His glance ran over her. 'You could benefit from some soothing therapy, you know. Being so uptight all the while can't be good for you. Ulcers, and that sort of thing. Very bad.' He shook his head sorrowfully.

Infuriating man. He probably did this sort of thing all the while. It was a way of life to him.

'Why don't you go and fish?' she gritted. With luck he might fall in and drown.

'Poor Lissa,' he murmured. 'You look cold out there. It must be the way the trees are shading out

the sun. Your nose has gone quite delightfully pink.'
He moved away from the door, and she heard him
clattering about inside the hut.

It was true; it was cooler on the island, and as the
afternoon progressed the temperature was likely to
drop even more. She had no idea how long he
intended to keep her here. By morning, if anyone
troubled to come looking for her, they would probably find her poor, frozen body rooted to the spot by
a cage of spindly icicles.

She peered through the open door. He was apply-
ing a match to some kind of heater, and from a small
counter in the far corner there was a distinct smell of
coffee pervading the atmosphere. He had rigged up
a primus stove, and a coffee-pot was already in
position. Her glance went to the shelves, where there
were enough stocks for a mini siege; dried milk,
bottled water, biscuits, soup.

He lifted a couple of mugs down from the shelf.
'Come and join me,' he suggested, tearing open a
pack of sugar. 'It isn't the Ritz, but at least there's
somewhere to sit, if you care to throw a cushion or
two on the bench.' He poured hot coffee into the
mugs and her nose twitched.

What she needed was a weapon of some sort,
something that would keep him at a distance should
the need arise. Her gaze skimmed over the fishing
rods and tackle that were stored neatly against the
side wall, and kept in place by a solid retaining bar.
A well-aimed butt-end, perhaps?

She sidled cautiously towards the equipment, and
perched on the edge of a deep mahogany box. How

dared he be so cool and confident, casually spooning powdered milk into the mugs, and stirring slowly, as if each task merited the utmost care and attention? He had no business being so much at ease while she was such a seething mass of insecurity.

He pushed a mug towards her. 'Do you want coffee?'

'I don't like helping myself to what isn't mine,' she muttered. 'Besides, I think I need something stronger.' Her jaw squared. 'You seem pretty familiar with this place. How often have you done this sort of thing? Don't you think the owner will have something to say about your making free with his belongings?'

He shrugged. 'Doesn't the fact that a pleasure is illicit make it more exciting?' He leaned against the counter, a smile tugging at his mouth. 'Haven't you lived dangerously, Lissa? Doesn't it make your blood sing to live on the wild side?'

'You're way off-beam,' she told him. 'I don't share your desire to skirt the seamy side of life.'

'I find that hard to believe. Those wide green eyes can't possibly be as innocent as they seem. Can't you recall even one reckless moment of devil-may-care?'

'I'd rather not,' she said with feeling, and he laughed softly, a husky, strangely pleasing sound that sent little quivers of sensation rippling along her spine.

'You are a beauty, though,' he murmured, his glance grazing her slender form. 'A jewel to tempt any man. I wonder——'

'Don't flirt with me, Deveraugh,' she cut in. 'I

don't know what's going on in your head, but I'm telling you now, if you have any ideas in that direction, you're on a loser.' Her gaze menaced him. 'You may enjoy playing those kinds of games, but count me out.'

He returned her stare. 'You prefer to play them with married men, don't you? They're much more your style. Or is it just the one in particular? Adam Franklyn? Shall I make a guess at his special appeal—could it be his money?' His expression was coldly cynical.

She frowned. Was this what lay behind the events of the afternoon? 'It appears you've already made up your mind,' she commented drily. 'So what if I'm involved in any way with Adam? What are you, judge and jury? Why should you be uneasy about the situation? Don't you have enough affairs of your own to occupy your mind?'

'I hate to see a decent man making a mess of his life. Adam and his wife are going through a difficult patch right now, and that's a great pity, because I believe they're well suited. They don't need someone like you to come along and wreak havoc.'

'Is Adam a friend of yours?' She examined the notion thoughtfully.

'Does that seem unlikely? A businessman and a man who puts up ramps for a living? What a snob you are, Lissa.'

'Not at all. I'm merely curious, since he's never mentioned you, and you show such an unflinching determination to interfere in his life.'

'I'm not inclined to stand by and watch a marriage-breaker in action. You spell trouble, and I want you out of the way.'

She said, with a flippancy she did not feel, 'Are you thinking in terms of hours, perhaps? Days, weeks? Permanent removal from the scene? Ought I to be fearful for my life?'

His mouth indented briefly. 'There are, as you pointed out, several options to take into consideration. Maybe not quite as extreme as the ones you mentioned. After all, even a hardened reprobate like myself must have some standards to adhere to. But there must be ways of dealing with women like you. It's just a question of finding the best one.'

She frowned. Was it true that Adam was having problems? Deveraugh was way out of line, but might there be some substance in what he was saying? Even so, his remarks about herself were uncalled for. A woman like her. . . To hear him talk, anyone would think she was some kind of Jezebel on the make.

She bit down on her annoyance. Arguing with him had about as much effect as a snowflake falling on a pond. She might just as well conserve her energy.

'You have it all wrong about Adam and myself,' she said, quite gently. 'There's really nothing between us. You're very much mistaken if you think that there is.'

Rourke nodded. 'That's why you were hugging each other.'

'I'm telling you the truth,' she persisted. 'Why won't you believe me?'

He swallowed the last of his coffee. 'It isn't me that

you have to persuade,' he told her, putting the mug down on the counter with a snap. 'It's his wife who's upset about the way things are going.'

'Was she there? I didn't see her with Adam.'

'It seems he was too busy to spend time with her.' He walked over to the neatly stacked rods and selected one, then bent to pick up a wicker fishing box from a corner of the room.

Lissa followed his actions with growing agitation. 'You're not seriously thinking of going fishing?' she demanded.

'I am.'

'But you can't. You have to take me back. I've told you, I'm not involved with Adam, and there's no reason for you to keep me here any longer.'

Rourke slung the broad strap of the wicker basket over one shoulder. 'So you say, but I have yet to be convinced. At any rate, another hour or so should allow time for Adam to realise you're not going to meet him. He can go home to his wife. I'm sure Emma will be more than happy to take your place.'

Lissa ground her teeth. 'You are the most obstinate, stubborn, pigheaded man I've ever had the misfortune to come across.'

'Not had a very wide experience, then, have you? I dare say that will change, though. There are bound to be other people who will object to letting you have your own way all the time. Stamp your feet, why don't you, Lissa? It'll make you feel better.'

About to batter the floor with her heel, Lissa stopped herself with a superhuman effort and held herself rigid. She would not give him the satisfaction.

Squaring her shoulders, she said tersely, 'I really don't see why I should have to explain myself to you. A man who goes in for abduction doesn't merit explanations, and neither,' she went on, warming to her subject, 'does anyone who can purloin other people's property, quite deliberately and without conscience, have any right to spout morals at me.'

'Your coffee's getting cold,' he said. 'If you don't want to come fishing, why don't you make yourself at home? I thought I spotted some magazines on that shelf.' Turning his back on her, he walked out of the cabin.

Lissa's slender fingers curled into fists at her sides. The man was insufferable, an egotistical, chauvinistic monster. How could he do this to her? How did he imagine he was going to get away with it?

She made an impatient sound. He didn't much care; that was the crux of the matter. Nothing she said seemed to make an iota of difference. He had made up his mind, and that was it.

Her gaze travelled after him. What was he, a one-man crusade? An hour, he'd said. OK, Mr Deveraugh, so be it. Maybe she'd play along with him for a while. But one hour was all he was going to get.

The magazines, strewn haphazardly over various sections of shelving, served to divert her temporarily. Whoever owned the cabin had wide-ranging interests—apart from several well-thumbed fishing journals and a variety of motoring magazines, there were numerous glossies that provided her with food for thought. She flicked her way through articles on planting sink gardens and handy tips for decorating a small flat, before her attention wandered.

She checked her watch. Thirty minutes. Hitching up her jacket collar, she went in search of him. For the remaining half-hour she would be pleasant to him, and then she would quietly and purposefully remind him of the time, and with gentle dignity insist that he take her home.

'Did you change your mind? Have you come to try your luck?' he asked in an undertone as she made an appearance beside him. Water lapped in desultory waves against the bank where he was sitting. 'They're just beginning to bite. See that carp in the keep net? It took me ten minutes to reel him in.'

'The poor thing must be exhausted,' she commented, keeping her voice low. One thing she knew was that you had to keep quiet around fish, or so men would have you believe. 'Do you do a lot of fishing round here? You seem to know all about the cabin.'

'I've been here a few times,' he admitted. 'I like to fish. It gives me time to mull things over, to get the world into perspective.'

'With your kind of work, I suppose you get plenty of opportunity.'

He shot her a sideways look. 'Meaning?'

She sat down beside him on the cool grass. 'Well, it can't be very secure, can it? From what I understood, the men are laid off more often than they are employed. Which means that you have plenty of time to cool your heels. . .and fish.'

There was no reason, of course, why a strong-bodied man like Rourke Deveraugh should be out of work for more than a day or so. She could think of all manner of jobs that he would be capable of doing . . .hewing rocks, digging for Siberian salt. . .

'It seems to bother you,' he reflected curiously, 'my work—or rather the lack of it. What is it, exactly, that disturbs you. . .? The fact that I can take pleasure in each day as it comes, that I don't churn myself up into a state of hyperactive neuroticism?'

'I couldn't live in such a haphazard way,' she told him. 'I like to know where my next meal is coming from, and that means I don't have time to sit around contemplating nature.'

'A determined businesswoman, out to succeed. I'm impressed.' He reeled in the line, flicking it deftly out of the water. 'You must have studied hard to get where you are today, starting up your own company. Drive and ambition—those are special qualities to come by.'

'Not really. If you wanted something badly enough, you could go after it.'

'Me?' Rourke looked faintly horrified. 'What would I want with ambition? Seems like a lot of hard work to me. I can't see the point of expending all that energy when I'm perfectly happy as I am.' He pulled the end of the nylon line towards him, reaching for the hook.

'But don't you feel you might be missing out on things?' Lissa found an odd fascination in watching the deft movements of his long, lean fingers. His hands were bronzed, they looked tough and capable.

'What could I possibly be missing? I can sit back

and watch the day go by, and when the float dips down in the water I know there's a fish pulling at the line. Then the adrenalin starts to pour, and the tussle is on.' His glance skimmed over her. 'Do you know that feeling, Lissa? Haven't you ever felt the simple pleasures of life, revelled in the purity of a lazy, self-seeking day?'

'Of course I have,' she answered, her gaze unconsciously wistful as she looked out over the smooth water of the lake. 'But there's so much to be done— businesses don't run themselves.'

'It's never a good thing to let the treadmill take you over,' he said firmly, examining the end of his line. 'Life can pass you by if you don't reach out and grab it. I'll bet,' he added, 'that for all your years of book-learning you know nothing about strapping on a pair of waders and getting out into the stream, feeling the water swirl around you—or how to bait a hook——' He pulled a small plastic box towards him. 'You could have a go now, if you wanted——'

Stricken by a sudden attack of acute and alarming panic, Lissa jumped to her feet. 'No—I don't think— I couldn't—I really don't want——' She paused for breath. 'I have to go, Deveraugh; it's time you took me home.'

'It can't be; we only just got here. Besides, this is the best time for fishing, when it's cooler—it makes them sluggish——'

'Easier for you to catch, you mean. Where's the sport in that?' Lissa argued. 'Anyway, you said an hour, and the time's up, I want to go back now.' She glanced over the assortment of floats and lead shot scattered on the ground beside him. 'Need any help with packing the gear away?'

He raised the tip of the rod, and gave the slightest flick of his wrist, swinging the line in a smooth curve out over the water. Lissa's eyes narrowed.

'Rourke,' she said carefully, 'it's cold out here, and I'd be grateful if you'd make a start in clearing up so that we can be on our way.'

'Cold?' he repeated. 'I hadn't noticed. Why don't you get a rod from the cabin and join me? The exercise will heat you up a bit. I'll put the bait on if you're squeamish.'

Her mouth tightened. 'You are clearly not listening to me. I said I want to go and I meant it. Are you going to take me home, or not?'

Leaning forward, his body stiffened suddenly as the bright orange float took a dive and disappeared from view. He said in a whisper. 'That's a bite; can you see it? Look, it's taking a nibble——' His concentration was total. Lissa watched, her mind beginning to tick over, like a little bomb, set to explode.

'Fishing is a cruel sport,' she said, her voice ominously taut.

'Not true,' he answered in hushed tones, absorbed by the darting movements of the float. 'They don't feel a thing, and I always put them back in the lake when I'm through.'

'Is that so?' She scanned the contents of the keep net with interest. 'In that case, I'll give you a hand.'

With the speed and precision of an avenging angel, she swooped up the net and tipped out the three squirming occupants, watching with grim satisfaction as they darted away.

'Now why did you have to go and do that?' Rourke demanded wrathfully. 'You've lost me the bite.'

'Good.' Lissa shook the water from her fingers. 'I'm cold, and I'm sick of waiting about out here. I'd appreciate it very much if you'd stash the gear in the box and get the boat started up.'

'Lissa, you're not——'

His voice followed her as she stomped back to the cabin, but she was not listening. It was too much. First he'd whisked her away without so much as a by-your-leave, and then he had blocked her meeting with Adam. Now he had the nerve to go back on his word. Plainly, he didn't know who he was dealing with. If he thought he could trample roughshod over her plans, just as he pleased, he had a lot to learn.

Putting the coffee-pot back on the primus to reheat the brew, she considered darkly that the simmering liquid was an accurate reflection of her own emotions. Talking to Rourke Deveraugh was like beating her head against a hard wooden post. It had no effect whatsoever, except to leave her feeling battered and thoroughly bad-tempered. She spooned extra sugar into her mug. She needed it.

A prickling sensation running the length of her spine told her that Rourke had made an appearance. She poured coffee and then glanced over in his direction. He was leaning against the door-jamb, his long body relaxed, his eyes faintly amused.

'I see you got around your scruples eventually,' he said.

She ignored him, taking a tentative sip from the hot liquid and savouring the moment as the warmth slowly invaded her limbs.

Pushing himself with indolent grace away from the door, Rourke came into the room and began to rummage about the shelves beneath the counter. He tugged out a small white bowl, and added water from a canister. Lissa watched as he began to wash his hands. No doubt he was going to raid the biscuits as well as everything else.

He tossed the packet towards her a few moments later. 'Want some?'

Her mouth twisted. 'No, thanks.' Putting her mug down, she rubbed her fingers along her arm and tried to chafe some heat into her cool flesh.

Rourke said, 'Still cold? The heater's a bit temperamental, but. . .' he grinned '. . .I could always warm you up, if you like?'

He started towards her and Lissa backed away, her eyes bright with fury. 'I don't like. Leave me alone.'

He held his hands up, palms flat, in a gesture of conciliation. 'It was only a suggestion. Why get so agitated about it?'

'That kind of suggestion I can do without.' Edging away from him, she felt her legs collide with the low shelving, and realised with a jolting shock that she had backed herself into a corner.

'Don't come any closer,' she warned, an unfamiliar panic rising in her throat. She was far too aware of him, of his tall, muscled frame just inches away from herself. He was too big, altogether too masculine— she could see the roughened texture of his tanned skin, and her senses were invaded by the subtle fragrance of his male cologne.

He was still moving, slowly coming forward, and in desperation she felt along the shelf behind her for some means of defence.

'What are you afraid of?' he asked. 'I've already told you that you're not in any danger.'

Her fingers closed on something hard and unyielding, like cold steel, and she jerked her hand upwards, thrusting the metal towards his chest. 'I mean it,' she said fiercely. 'Keep away.'

Rourke stared down at the place where the menacing point of the scissors threatened his solar plexus. He said carefully, 'I hope you don't intend using those on me, Lissa. I bleed easily. Why don't you put them down? Believe me, you don't need that kind of protection.'

'I'll decide what I need.' She made a frantic gesture with the sharpened blades and at the same moment Rourke went into action. It happened so fast that her mind went into a spin, and she reeled dizzily, her gaze unfocused. An iron band clamped her wrist, her arm was forced backwards as Rourke's hard body slammed against her, knocking the air from her lungs. There was a moment of profound, intense stillness, and in the breathless silence that followed she became aware of the heavy thumping of her heart against her ribcage, the rapid, quick-fire beat of her pulse. He must have felt it too—how could he not when he was so close; how could he fail to pick up the reckless drumming of her senses?

He said slowly, 'You don't know me very well,

Lissa, or you would understand that I don't take kindly to facing the wrong end of a pair of shears. That can definitely be counted as one of the worst moves you ever made.'

Trapped against the hard edge of the wooden shelving by the taut pressure of his muscled thighs, the folly of her panicked action was borne in on her with devastating precision. She dared not move. With a harsh clatter, the scissors fell from her lifeless fingers and skidded across the floor.

'That's better,' he said. 'Now maybe we could calm things down a bit.'

'You started it.'

'I did no such thing.'

'You brought me here against my will,' she accused him hotly, enraged by his denial, 'and now you're manhandling me. You're not giving me room to breath —I shall probably expire through suffocation. And if I do escape extinction I shall most likely be black and blue from this wood digging into my back—and I shouldn't be surprised if you've broken my wrist.'

Releasing her, he said, 'For someone who's supposedly about to breathe her last, you appear to have an awful lot to say for yourself. I doubt very much that your wrist is even slightly reddened, let alone broken. What did you expect of me? Did you imagine I'd stand passively by while you used me for bayonet practice?' He scanned her thoughtfully. 'Yes, you probably did. Are you always this explosive?'

'Stick around and you'll find out,' she predicted tautly, rubbing at her wrist. 'You think that you can do just as you like—well, you're wrong.'

'In that case,' he murmured, 'I might as well go back to my fishing. Since my presence seems to be provoking you to acts of wild aggression, I think it would be best to leave you in peace for a while. No doubt you could do with some time to reflect on things.'

'Don't you dare walk off and leave me here,' she commanded fiercely. 'I thought we just establised that it was time to start back?'

'Did we? I'm in no particular hurry. Besides, I'd much prefer more conducive company if I'm to travel down river. With you aboard, I wouldn't dare turn my back for fear of becoming fish meal.'

'Don't be ridiculous!' she exclaimed. 'You know very well that was just a—a flash-in-the-pan reaction—I felt threatened—it was just self-defence.'

He inclined his dark head briefly. 'When you feel less. . .threatened. . .a couple of hours, perhaps—I'll take you back.' He walked away, his long, easy stride taking him down the rough path to the lakeside.

Lissa stared angrily after his departing figure, a turbulent storm gathering momentum in her green eyes. He had no right to treat her this way. Who did he think he was? Well, enough was enough. There had to be some way of putting an end to his domineering activities. So he thought she was explosive, did he? She smiled thinly. He had better look out. She would show him what it meant to rouse a sleeping volcano.

Skirting the lakeside, she took a route which led her in the opposite direction from him. She needed time to think, to decide what to do. Where were those dark Plutonian forces when she needed them to aid and abet her plotting?

If only there was some other means of getting away from this place. Surely, if this was a regular haunt for whoever owned the cabin, there would be another boat somewhere? A simple row-boat, perhaps? Didn't fishermen like to go out into the middle of lakes to fish? It was a long shot, of course, but if she looked carefully she might find something.

It took half an hour before she came across it, moored by a small wooden landing stage. It was only borrowing, she told herself. As soon as she had achieved her purpose, she would see that the boat was returned. Her lips curved. Now for Mr Rourke Deveraugh.

What was the best method of disabling a motor boat, temporarily, at least? A length of wire wound around the rudder? Messy, but no doubt it would be effective. There had been a coil of wire in the cabin, she felt sure. Along with a pair of waders. And candles. Hadn't she noticed a box on one of the shelves? What about candle wax in the key slot? Or water in the fuel tank? There must be all sorts of things she could try.

Some time later, she made her way back to where he had been sitting. He was still fishing, the line plumbing the depths of the water, gently swaying in the light breeze. At peace with his world. A smile curved her lips. Not for long, though. This particular fish was very shortly going to find itself in exceedingly troubled waters.

He turned as she approached, watching her cautiously. It was the scissors that held his attention, probably. He stood up, wedging the rod against the wicker box.

'Lissa?'

'Deveraugh.' Her greeting was warm, light. She felt oddly happy, unconcerned. Glancing over the line as it arced over the lake, her eyes took on a faintly emerald glow. She walked to the water's edge. 'How's the fishing going?'

'Well enough.' His gaze was very steady, totally concentrated.

She nodded. 'We can change that.' Leaning forward towards the nylon line, she snipped with the scissors.

'What the——?' He rushed to inspect the scene of desecration, and she told herself that the opportunity was simply too good to miss. He was far too close to the edge, he might have slipped anyway, and what did it matter if she added just a little extra impetus? With a bright flicker of satisfaction, she watched him slide down into the water, his large body making a flurry of waves ripple the surface.

Elation fizzed through her veins. It had been so easy. Surveying the results of her handiwork, she stayed only long enough to see him scrabble for the safety of the bank. He was not unduly damaged, only very, very wet. And furious.

She laughed in the face of his anger, then turned and ran, fleet-footed, to where she had moored the row-boat. Pulling away into the stream, she reflected happily that vengeance was oh, so sweet.

He turned as she approached, watching her reaction. It was the scenes that hurt this audience, probably. He stood there watching the rest, biting the inside of his cheek.

CHAPTER THREE

ADAM'S secretary was engrossed in totting up a column of figures when Lissa walked into his office on Monday morning. Looking up as Lissa approached the desk, she pushed long pink-tipped fingers through the silky mass of her fair hair, a frown shading her blue eyes.

'May I help you?' she asked.

'I'd like a word with Adam,' Lissa said. 'Is he around?'

'He's rather busy—you've come at a bad time, I'm afraid, Miss Holbrook. I could pass on a message for you.'

'I don't think so. I'll wait, if you'd just let him know I'm here.'

Rebecca Charlesworth's hesitation was only slight. 'Of course. Perhaps you'd care to take a seat.'

Lissa wandered over to the window and gazed out over the expanse of carefully tended shrubbery that bordered the car park. In the distance, she could see the field where Saturday's fête had taken place, devoid now of tents and stands. There was no evidence of car ramps, and all the rafts had long since disappeared. It was as though the events of the weekend might never have happened, had been wiped away.

'Sweetheart, it's good to see you again.' She swung

48

round as Adam came towards her. 'I looked for you after the raft procession, but you were nowhere to be seen.'

'I wanted to apologise for that,' she said. 'I'd explain, but it's a long story, and I know you're busy. I hoped, though, that you wouldn't mind if I stopped by this morning? Or is it inconvenient?'

'Actually, you've come at just the right moment. We're having trouble with the new computer. I wonder if you might give Becky a hand to sort it out while you're here? I've had a look at it, but I can't find why it isn't working. Knowing what a talent you have for these things, you'll probably have it sorted out in two ticks.'

'I'll do my best,' she agreed, and he smiled his relief.

'You're a wonderful girl. What would I do without you? I'm in the middle of things right now, but we should be able to snatch a word in half an hour if that's OK with you? Better still, why don't you come along to a party we're throwing tomorrow evening? It's a get-together for some of our clients and their wives, and hopefully for prospective customers, too. You might come away with a few commissions of your own.'

'I like the sound of that. Thanks.' She returned his smile. 'All this industry must be a sign of things looking good.'

He grimaced. 'It has its ups and downs, though. This morning we seem to be having nothing but problems.'

'Let's see if I can help, shall we?' Walking back to Rebecca's cluttered desk, she set to work.

'You're a genius Lissa,' Adam told her a few minutes later. 'I knew you could do it. Remind me to give you a big kiss some time.' His fingers circled her arms, gripping her lightly. 'Be sure and come to the party tomorrow, won't you? I'll jot the address down for you.'

'I will. I'll look forward to it.'

'What's going on?' A deep, shockingly familiar voice made them both turn and look towards the door. 'What is she doing here?'

Lissa's stomach made a strange somersault. She was asking herself the same question. What was *he* doing here, of all places? Hadn't she thought she'd seen the last of Rourke Deveraugh? He stood in the doorway, leaning against the frame, frowning darkly, and Adam broke away from her guiltily under that frosty stare.

Her gaze scanned the expensively tailored cut of his dark suit, the white shirt, faintly striped, the immaculate cuffs. The nape of her neck began to prickle. Where was the man of the casual clothes and easy manner? Something was very wrong. This man was a grim-faced stranger, his eyes cold with anger, like chips of blue ice. He bore no relation to the man she'd had the misfortune to come into contact with at the weekend. And exactly what was his connection with Adam?

'Rourke——' Adam greeted him with enthusiasm, drawing Lissa forward to meet him. 'You remember the girl I was telling you about? This is Lissa, Lissa Holbrook——'

'We've already met.' Rourke's sharp tone cut him

short. 'I can't say that the experience was one to savour.' His cold glance slid over her. 'I'm glad to have caught up with you again so soon, Miss Holbrook. It saves me the trouble of going after you. There are one or two things you and I have to settle.'

Adam scanned his taut features, uncomfortable and slightly puzzled by the undercurrent of tension that had suddenly sprung up. 'I wasn't aware that you knew each other.' Taking a folder from a wire tray on the desk, he said, 'I've been trying to reach you all morning.'

'I've been at the Brooksby plant,' Rourke informed him briskly. 'There was a foul-up in dispatch.' He looked at Lissa as though it was all her doing, and she sent him a poisonous stare in return.

'Things aren't too good here either,' Adam said. 'The new production quotas have stirred up a hornet's nest—and that's without the added difficulty of a flu epidemic.'

'And one or two cases of Monday-morning syndrome, I shouldn't doubt.' Rourke's jaw tightened, a muscle flicking irritably in his cheek.

'Something will have to be sorted out—and quickly,' Adam muttered, whisking up a pile of paperwork from a tray on the polished surface of a desk. 'If we can't get these orders out on time, all the effort we've put in will have been for nothing. Customers will start going somewhere else.'

'That's hardly likely to happen,' Rourke denied curtly, his icy gaze raking mercilessly over Lissa's slender figure. Her shoulders went back, her spine stiffening. He wasn't going to intimidate her. 'We haven't worked all these months to have it go up in smoke now,' he said. His fingers drummed on the door-frame. 'We could offer the men unlimited over-time—put them on bonus. It might be worth con-sidering a profit-sharing scheme. That could get the ball rolling again.'

Adam tapped the papers against his knuckles. 'That sounds like a good idea. There'll have to be a union meeting. Are you going to come in on that?'

Rourke scowled. 'You can deal with it, can't you? Unless there are any snags, I want to get back to the workshop. This new hoist I'm working on needs modifications. There have been enough delays already.'

Adam nodded, his mouth making a wry twist, and Lissa murmured, 'I'd better be on my way. I've one or two calls to make.' She wasn't going to stay around and bandy words with Deveraugh.

'Not so fast,' Rourke gritted, soft menace underly-ing those laconic syllables. 'As I said, you and I have a few things to settle before you leave.' Sharp blue eyes impaled her.

'Have we? What a bore. I really have more import-ant things to attend to.' She contemplated walking out anyway, but she was loath to create a scene in the office. How far would she get, after all? That piercing gaze threatened immediate reprisal, the tough, unyielding stance of his hard body blocked her path and intimidated her. He meant business. She would not put it past him to use force.

She studied him with resentment. She did not know him now, did not recognise that steel thread of arrogant command. This was a man of authority, a man of power, who had only to speak and everybody around him flew into action.

He was not at all what he seemed, she reflected bitterly. Saturday had merely been a run-in; she could see it now. He had been toying with her that day on the river, playing games to satisfy some peculiar quirk of his character.

How could she have got him so wrong? This was no fish, no easy prey. No, this was a shark, a deadly, multi-toothed shark, and he was homing in on her with lethal precision.

'I'm glad you thought better of it,' he said tersely, and turned his attention to the secretary, who was staring in a distracted fashion at the computer print-out.

'What's wrong, Rebecca?'

The woman gave a nervous start, her hands jerking in a little, agitated movement. 'I—it's nothing—the—the tabulation's come out uneven—I'll have to do it again.'

'Do it after lunch. You'll think more clearly after you've had a break.'

'Oh, no. I've far too much to do—I've all the——'

'Go to lunch, Rebecca.' His voice was clipped. It was an order, a decree that had to be obeyed, and the woman obviously knew better than to argue. She raked a hand through her fine blonde hair.

Adam said. 'I'll give you a lift into town if you want, Becky. I have to pay a visit to the wholesaler, so I could drop you off and pick you up later to bring you back. Just come over to the production office when you're ready. I've a couple of things to sort out, then we can be off.'

'Thank you.' Rebecca went in search of her bag, and Lissa sent an irate look in Adam's direction. How could he think of abandoning her to the malevolent clutches of this voracious monster?

'Adam——'

'I have to go, Lissa, I've just remembered something I have to collect urgently—but I can see that you and Rourke have one or two things to say to each other, anyway.' He reached for a piece of notepaper. 'Don't forget our date,' he reminded her, scribbling down an address and thrusting it into her hand. 'Sorry to rush off.' He made for the door, sweeping out of the office with Rebecca in tow, stopping only to add as an afterthought, 'Ignore Rourke's bad temper. He hates days when he can't get straight into his workshop. He won't bite.'

'Don't be too sure of that,' Rourke advised nastily as the door closed on his two colleagues. 'The way I feel about you right now, I might just be tempted to snap your bones into little pieces.' He bared his teeth, and Lissa could almost feel their sharp incision on her skin. He was manifestly rattled about the dousing he had received at her hands.

'I'm not afraid of you,' she said. 'You had it coming. If you think you can abduct people without penalty, it simply goes to show how off-track you are.'

'I might sue for damages,' he threatened with vindictive relish, disregarding her complaint. 'What you did to that boat was only marginally less criminal than what you tried to do to me. Assault, attempted murder by drowning, damage to property——'

'Self-defence,' she put in tightly, 'a slight dampening when you overbalanced. What a shame your line broke. I do hope you had a spare reel.'

'I'd advise you, lady,' he said with grim emphasis, 'to keep a check on that flippant tongue of yours. I may yet decide to take matters into my own hands. Far more satisfying than letting the law take its ponderous course.' He walked over to a door at the far end of the office and flung it open. 'Come through,' he ordered, motioning with a brief jerk of his head.

Her glance skittered in the opposite direction towards the exit.

'Don't think you can skulk off,' he growled. 'I haven't finished with you yet, and don't imagine I wouldn't enjoy dragging you back. Since you left me so abruptly, my mind has been teeming with a whole variety of things I'd like to do to you.'

She viewed him with dislike. She didn't doubt he was quite capable of putting his words into action. He'd already kidnapped her once, hadn't he? Perhaps it would be wise to pander a little to his whims since it seemed he was prone to these Viking tendencies. Appearing cool and calm would be difficult, but it was the only way to deal with this man. She would not let him get under her skin.

'You lied to me,' she said, her voice laced with accusation as she walked through to what appeared to be a workshop. Surfaces were cluttered with an assortment of electronic equipment, and mechanical contrivances in varied states of readiness. A blue and white mug, half filled with cold coffee, weighted down a stack of papers. 'You were never a member of that stunt team.' She fixed him with a glittering emerald stare.

'I don't recall saying that I was.' He flicked a switch on the percolator, which was set up in a recess above one of the work-benches, and reached for a fresh mug.

'You let me go on believing that you were one of their crew,' she persisted heatedly, provoked by his bland unconcern. 'That counts as a lie in my book.'

'Then your book needs some adjustment. If you choose to jump to conclusions, that's your problem, not mine.'

She smiled grimly. 'Think again, Mr Deveraugh, why don't you? You were quite happy to sink yourself in the role I gave you. Doesn't that seem a little odd, even to you? If you prefer a world of fantasy to real life, maybe you should see someone about it. You may need help.'

'And you don't, I suppose? You'd be wise, Miss Holbrook, to keep a firm control on your own lively imagination. The consequences of indulging it might not be at all to your liking. There's still the strong possibility you might find yourself in court over your actions this weekend, and I can tell you that judges take a poor view of women who imagine themselves potential victims. Assaulting an innocent companion on a fishing trip is not something that will be viewed lightly.'

'How dare you?' she demanded, forcing the words

out through her teeth. 'How can you twist everything around like that?'

'Twist?' he murmured silkily, one dark brow lifting. 'Isn't that how it was? It certainly seemed that way to me. Besides——' his mouth took on a sardonic curve '—what price would you put on your credibility—a woman who liaises with a married man, makes dates with him behind his wife's back? You don't believe in wasting any time, do you? First chance, and you're hanging around him again.' He paused, eyeing her with distaste. 'That's the one characteristic about you that might in fact be positive. You don't give up, do you? You stick right in there, to the bitter end.'

'It was business,' she retorted coldly. 'We were talking business.'

His eyes darkened with scepticism. 'It didn't look very businesslike when I walked in.'

'Why don't you ask him?'

'He'd deny it. He already mentioned that a girlfriend was back in town. Wonderful woman, he said, great legs.' His glance skimmed over her slender frame, the deep, plum-coloured suit with its tailored jacket and contrasting beige silk blouse, the shapely, slim-fitting skirt. 'He was right about the legs, anyway.'

Lissa glared at him. 'Your arrogance is so potent, I wonder that you don't bottle it.'

Rourke looked at her thoughtfully. 'From what I understand, you broke off your romance with him and went off to university to pursue your qualifications. That could have been the cause of all the trouble, I suppose. Things were left unsettled between you. Then, in the years that you were away, he met Emma and married her. You couldn't cope with that.'

'Rot,' she said with caustic vehemence. 'You're getting things completely out of proportion. I'd had enough of working in an accounts department, my family had uprooted themselves, and I thought it was time for a change. I was a little late in deciding what I wanted to do with my life, but my decision had nothing to do with Adam. To hear you talk, anyone would think I was some kind of wanton, a man-stealer. If it didn't make me so angry it would be laughable.'

Rourke looked at her through narrowed eyes. 'Wasn't there an episode with a company director before Adam?' he queried, his voice deceptively soft. 'A *married* company director who was also your employer? Or do I have that wrong as well?'

Lissa stared, her face whitening, her expression stunned. 'How did you—what makes you think——?'

'I believe Adam may have mentioned it. A blight on your past, a time you would rather not remember. . .' There was mockery now in those piercing blue eyes.

She said tersely, 'It seems to me that Adam has had far too much to say for himself. That never used to be a fault of his, running off at the mouth. It must be your noxious influence.'

'I shouldn't let it bother you unduly, Lissa,' he murmured. 'We all make mistakes at some time or other. You can't spend the rest of your life paying for them. And, when all's said and done, there's not much wrong with a little wantonness here and there. It adds spice to life, don't you agree?' He moved towards her, his gaze speculative. 'The only pity is that you concentrate your attention on men who are already spoken for. Why not make a change, focus on me instead? I'm sure we could do well together, despite your scorpion tongue. Who knows? Ahead of us might lie a future of delight and discovery, a sparkling fountain of new experiences.'

'Another wild fantasy,' she responded with cool disdain. 'You'd do well to rid yourself of those kind of notions, Deveraugh, or you could find yourself greatly disappointed.'

She cast a last fleeting look around the room. 'And now,' she said in curt dismissal, 'as I can see that you have an awful lot to do around here. . .' she gave the dirty coffee-mug a disapproving look '. . . I shall leave you to get on with it. You never know, you might find that work is a grand panacea.' Flicking back her head with a haughty toss of bright auburn curls, she walked to the door and flung it open.

Rourke's voice came after her. 'You haven't escaped, you know. Enjoy the fragile illusion of freedom while you can, but remember—I'm on your trail. I'll be right behind you, following your every move.'

She continued walking. She did not look back. The arrogant effrontery of the man defied belief.

* * *

The address Adam had given her was relatively easy to find. Set against the verdant tracery of mature trees, and the glinting spread of a glassy lake in the background, the house took on a warm roseate glow in the fading light of the evening sun. It was a well-proportioned house, Lissa decided, the lines drawn with an unfailing eye for symmetry and beauty.

Carefully bringing her low-slung MG to a halt on the gravelled drive, she found herself once again debating the vexed question of Adam's relationship with Rourke.

Obviously there was some kind of partnership involved, but it seemed to her that Adam did most of the running of the outfit. Perhaps Rourke was there as an ideas man—certainly he didn't show much enthusiasm for getting into the nitty-gritty of the day-to-day workload. Typical. It was what she might have expected. Hadn't he taken a day off to go fishing, while Adam busied himself with prospective clients?

It had been Adam, too, who had broached the subject of a new computer programming system for the business. He wouldn't have done that, would he, if he wasn't holding the reins. . .? So it looked as though there was little reason for her to think of backing out of the deal they were planning.

Perhaps this evening they might be able to sort out the details. Stepping out of the car, she smoothed down the skirt of her flame-coloured dress, and began to walk towards the house.

'Lissa,' Adam greeted her at the door. 'I'm glad you made it.' He stood back and urged her inside.

'Come on in. I'd introduce you to my wife, but she's disappeared for the umpteenth time this evening. Help yourself to a drink from the bar. I'll be back in a second—I have to go and see to the hors-d'oeuvres—management's orders.'

Armed with a glass of red wine, Lissa let her gaze wander around. The lounge was long, and wide, L-shaped, the luxurious furnishings reflecting the cool, serene hues of the sea. The room was crowded, the hub of conversation mingling with the soft strains of music that issued from overhead speakers.

'Well, well. If it isn't the green-eyed temptress herself.'

Her breath snagged in her throat. Rourke of course; she had known he would be here, hadn't she? She was prepared—wasn't her armour in place, intact? She felt, intuitively, that it had to be. In some dark, indefinable way, Rourke Deveraugh was dangerous to her. In the depths of her soul she knew it, knew that he could hurt her, badly.

'And the renegade,' she murmured coolly. 'How strange to come across you in a civilised setting such as this. I'm sure you'd be far more at home somewhere on the high seas with a scarf around your head and a cutlass at your belt.'

'I see your claws are as sharp as ever.' His glance flashed over her, his mouth making a cynical line. 'You look bewitchingly lovely, as usual. But that's all part of the lure, isn't it? An exotic beauty, with fire at her heart, a flame that could easily devour an unwary man. What a good thing I know you for what you are. But tell me, why are you here, Lissa? Have you come to torment your victim, drive him out of his head? Poor Adam. With his wife at hand, what will he do?'

'I'm sure Adam will have no difficulty in doing exactly as he pleases, which at the moment happens to be attending to his guests.' She smiled thinly. 'Why don't you go and help him out? He mentioned prospective clients. I'm sure you could make yourself useful—if you tried hard enough.'

'Are you trying to get rid of me?' Rourke's voice held a note of derision. 'I warned you, you won't find that so easy. I'm on to you, and I intend to spike your little game. Don't imagine you can play me for a fool. Adam may have fallen for your charms, but I've got a clear head and I'm immune.'

'I'm glad to hear it,' she said with cold contempt. 'It means you won't be disappointed when I choose to ignore you.' Purposefully, she moved away from him, determined to put some distance between them.

At the far end of the room, close to where tables had been laid with an appetising buffet, she noticed a smooth archway. Circuiting the crowd that milled around with plates and dishes in search of sustenance, she walked towards it, and saw that it led into a pleasingly arranged conservatory. The room was empty, and she went in, thankful that Rourke had not followed her.

Slowly, her pulse returned to normal. She could not understand the effect he had on her. It was very odd, this way he had of dragging all her senses into screaming vitality.

Her glance went around the room. Diffused lighting cast a warm amber glow over a couple of oak display cabinets and reflected off the glass-panelled walls. Curiosity drew her forward to explore. A driftwood carving, illuminated in a small alcove, caught her attention, and she went over to take a closer look. Absorbed, she studied the intricacies of the twists and curves.

'Unusual design, isn't it?'

Startled, she turned and recognised with a swift sinking sensation the tall figure of Richard Blake. Her first employer. Her first love.

'I. . . Yes, I haven't seen anything quite like this before.' Drawing in a silent, deep breath, she braced herself and said, 'How are you, Richard? It's been a long time.'

'I'm fine, thank you. I must say, you're looking well, Lissa. Running your own firm must agree with you.'

'It does.' She paused, and was driven to add, 'But then, working for you was all the incentive I needed. You made me think more clearly about what I wanted from life.'

He grimaced. 'So you ran away.'

Lissa shrugged. 'I wouldn't put it quite that way. I was twenty years old, after all. There had to come a point where I took control of my future.'

'Things shouldn't have ended the way they did, Lissa. You didn't give me time——'

'You had more than enough time, Richard,' she said drily. 'If I'd known you were married, you wouldn't have had any at all. You strung me a line, and I was naïve enough to fall for it. Lucky for me that I got out before you could entice me into the ultimate folly of going to bed with you.'

She took a sip of the red wine, letting it roll around her tongue, savouring it slowly. The action gave her the moments she needed to adjust, to assess her own feelings. Coming face to face with him after all this time had been a shock; she had not known quite how she would react. Strangely, it was not nearly as traumatic as she had imagined.

'I behaved abominably,' he said. 'I realise that. At the time——'

'It doesn't matter any more.' Her fingers tightened on the stem of her glass, twisting it experimentally. Her chin lifted. 'That's all in the past. Since then I've made a new start.'

Richard ran a thumb diffidently along the lines of the carving. 'I'd like us to be friends,' he said, his voice low, his face close to hers. 'Is that possible?'

Lissa shrugged. 'All things are possible.'

A sound from the doorway made them both turn. Rourke lounged negligently against the wall.

'What a cosy scene. Am I interrupting anything?' He did not look as though the thought bothered him much.

Richard sprang away from Lissa, his skin flushing a dull red. 'We were just talking,' he muttered.

Rourke's mouth quirked upwards. 'Of course. What else would you be doing, tucked away in a moonlit conservatory with a beautiful woman?' His eyes narrowed thoughtfully. 'Aren't you a little off territory, Blake? I hadn't expected to see you here this evening.'

'Because we're in the same line of business, you mean?' Richard shrugged with some diffidence. 'I'm not about to poach orders, if that's what you had in mind. Adam invited me along. We were at college together, but perhaps you already know that?'

Rourke nodded. 'Old friendships die hard, don't they? From what I've heard, you and Lissa go back some years, too. I imagine it wouldn't have taken her long to captivate you. It seems to be quite a talent she has.'

Lissa threw him a malevolent scowl. 'A talent sadly lacking in you. I doubt you could captivate a leech.'

Rourke lifted a dark brow. 'You seem a little touchy, sweetheart. Is something wrong?'

'Nothing that your absence wouldn't cure. As a matter of fact, we were having a private conversation in here. Perhaps you're too thick-skinned to notice.'

'My apologies,' he intoned gravely. 'I'd hate to disturb you. You must have a lot of catching up to do. And, after all, Adam *is* still busy.'

He turned and walked out of the room, his laughter echoing softly through the air.

Richard cleared his throat. 'He knew all about you and me. Is there anything that man doesn't know?'

Lissa did not answer. Whatever he knew, he always looked on the black side, judged her and found her wanting. It was an infuriating trait, and it made her blood boil every time he came near. What she would give to punch him on the nose, and flatten once and for all his insulting, devilish assumptions.

Richard said, 'What did he mean about Adam being busy?'

Looking down, she found that her fingers were tightly clenched. Slowly, with an effort, she unlocked them. 'Forget it. He's obviously in a boorish mood.'

He gave a rueful nod. 'I take it there's no love lost between you two.'

'None at all.' It was an understatement.

He drew in a breath, his shoulders going back. 'You know, Lissa, seeing you tonight has made me realise that I'd hate to lose contact with you again. 'How would you feel about working with me once more?'

Her look was frankly cynical. 'You have to be joking,' she said.

'No.' He shook his head. 'I'm serious about this. Hear me out, please. I meant—would you consider developing a program for my company? We're expanding rapidly, and it's imperative that we function with more efficiency. I know you could come up with something—your work was always the best, and I've every faith that you could do a good job.'

She regarded him thoughtfully for a moment or two. Raising her glass to her lips, she took another sip of the wine. She suspected his motives in asking her. Was he trying to rake over old coals? For some years she had struggled to come to terms with her own emotions. Always, in the background, in the dim recesses of her mind, there had been that niggling doubt. Was there a chance that those painful feelings could surface once more if she met him again?

Now, at last, she realised that whatever she had felt for Richard was long since buried, under an avalanche of hurt and disillusion. She had thought herself in love, but it had been only an infatuation, the awakening response of a young, impressionable girl.

'Will you do it?' he urged. 'I'd pay you the top rate.'

Her glance was cool. 'I'd make certain you did.'

'Does that mean you'll work with me?'

'I haven't decided.'

Lissa put down her half-empty glass on a wide, oak-timbered shelf, and mulled over his proposition. Her instincts told her that if she was to survive in the world of industry and commerce she had to push the past to one side, and get on with life. She was a professional; she couldn't afford to let opportunities pass. Whatever problems came up, she could handle them, one at a time.

She said, 'You understand that whatever there was between us is over? Finished, gone.'

Richard swallowed, then nodded slowly. 'I know; I accept that now. I fought against it, but when you went away, and stayed away, despite all my letters and calls, I knew that there was never going to be any chance for me.'

'Then as long as that's quite clear I'll see what I can do to plan out a program for you. I'll make arrangements with your secretary. Now, if you'll excuse me, I have to go and speak to Adam.' She left the room, conscious all the time of Richard's devouring gaze.

In the lounge, people were clustered around, chatting easily to one another, and she moved among them, stopping now and again to talk to friends. It was some minutes later when her glance encountered Rourke, engrossed in conversation.

He was with a woman, of course. The same woman who had been with him on Saturday. She was gazing up at him earnestly, a haunted, troubled quality about her expression, marring the beautiful lines of her oval-shaped face. Her fingers clutched at the light material of his jacket sleeve as though imploring him to listen.

Don't waste your time, she silently advised the young woman. He isn't the type to be tied down, even by the flimsiest of bonds.

She watched as Rourke bent his head closer to his companion. His arm went around her, squeezing gently, a reassuring, comforting gesture. Lissa felt her stomach muscles tighten, and turned away.

She found Adam by the bar, munching on a sausage roll, his plate piled high with tempting savouries. 'You have the appetite of a horse,' she told him, and he gave her an answering grin.

'I need it,' he said, wiping crumbs from his mouth. 'I burn up masses of calories.'

'That's because you're never still. Trying to snatch a word with you is like trying to hold on to a fistful of quicksilver.'

His smile was rueful. 'So Emma keeps telling me. It's just that there's always so much to do.'

'You mean you're a workaholic, you can't resist the temptation. Take five minutes and tell me what it is you want me to do for Lynx. By the time I'm finished, you might be so organised you'll even be able to find time for your wife.'

'Now that idea holds definite appeal.' He picked up a cocktail sausage and gave it a light flourish. 'Let me outline what's happening with the firm at present and you can begin to gather your thoughts.'

He launched into a detailed explanation, punctuated with stolen bites at the food on his plate, and Lissa followed his words with careful absorption, nodding occasionally. It did not seem that the task would be too difficult.

'I doubt there'll be too many problems,' she told him. 'Given access to the data back at your office, I should be able to come up with a suitable package.'

'That's good.' He swallowed the last of his lager and contemplated his empty glass. 'Can I get you some more wine?'

She shook her head. 'No, thanks, I have some somewhere.' Glancing around while Adam negotiated a refill for himself, her gaze was drawn involuntarily back to Rourke. The dark-haired woman was nowhere to be seen, but he was not alone.

He was dancing, now, with Rebecca, his arms entwined loosely around her slim waist, their bodies moving in slow motion to the lazy beat of the music. Rebecca was smiling, responding to something he had said. They both looked relaxed, an easy familiarity between them now that they were away from the office and cut free from the restrictions of boss and secretary.

Lissa's eyes darkened. She had been right in her summing-up of him. He was a flirt. It wasn't the fault of the women he was with. He was dangerously attractive—anyone could see that—a tall, lean figure in dark, smoothly fitting trousers that emphasised that taut muscularity of his thighs. His dark jacket hung open to reveal a finely striped shirt, unbuttoned at the neck so that she could see the healthy bronze of his skin.

She clamped her teeth. He was an out-and-out profligate, darting from one partner to the next. Now he was exercising his charm on Rebecca. What was his relationship with that woman anyway? Just how involved were they?

Her fingers clenched into the soft material of her flame-coloured dress, crushing the delicate fabric. Of course it didn't bother her personally. She wasn't jealous; of course she wasn't. How could she feel such deep emotions for a man who riled her so easily? It was anger she felt. Dislike.

Restlessly, she looked away. Adam was talking to a man she vaguely recognised as a financier of some sort, and she wondered when it might be possible to leave without appearing rude. She had no wish to stay and watch Rourke with his various women.

For a few minutes longer, she mingled with the crowd, exchanging a word here and there. Adam had been right about the contacts she could make, but her mind was no longer in tune with business this evening. Perhaps she would go and finish her wine, and then make her escape. Another half-hour or so, perhaps, and she could be free.

The conservatory was still empty, the lamps burning low, the moon casting long silver shadows over the terrace beyond the wide patio doors. Stars glittered with the brilliance of jewels against a velvet backcloth.

She went over to the shelf where she had left her drink, and stared down in dismay at the overturned glass, the shards of crystal glinting wickedly up at her in the dim light. Wine spilled out in a small pool, red and dark, like a bloodstain creeping out over the burnished timber. There was a square envelope, stark, white, propped up against the wall, with her name printed in bold black lettering across the front. She stared at it for a long time, shivering, icy fingers trailing along her spine.

At last, shakily, she picked up the envelope and ripped it open, taking out the single sheet of paper. Her hand trembled and she clamped it hard against her chest until the attack of nerves had subsided a little. After a minute or so, when she felt stronger, she opened out the paper and stared down at the message printed there.

At your peril you reject what the stars foretell. Danger stalks this place, and you alone are its quarry. Go back to where you came from, Lissa Holbrook, or read your destiny in spilt wine.

Lissa crumpled the paper into her clammy palm. All at once she couldn't breathe. The air in her lungs was stifling, fear rising in her throat like hordes of butterfly wings clamouring for release, choking her. The lurking menace of those few sinister lines hung over her like a sentence of doom, an ominous harbinger of death and destruction.

Panic swept through her. She had to get out of

here. Rushing towards the glass doors, she fumbled with frantic haste at the catch. She had to get out of this room, out of this house, or she would surely suffocate.

The heavy panels gave way at last beneath her fingers and she lurched out on to the terrace, crossed it, then raced over the wide sweep of lawn. The paper dropped from her fingers, blown across the grounds by a light breeze, but she ignored it. She ran, fleeing the demons that pursued her, dragging in great gasps of cold air as if they were her last. A stitch seared her side and she came to a stumbling halt, pressing her palms to the painful place, waiting until the sharp sting had eased a little. Then slowly she straightened, her eyes focusing on her dark surroundings.

A lake. The gently wavering fronds of a willow tree. And Adam. She couldn't see him too clearly, but it was Adam, wasn't it? A tall, dark figure in the shadows, leaning against the bole.

She had startled him with her headlong flight. 'Lissa?' he queried softly, his voice muffled. 'What are you doing out here? Is something wrong?'

She did not answer, silent tears of relief coursing down her cheeks. She ran to him, wrapping her arms around his chest, and burying her cheek against the solid comfort of his ribcage. For a moment, he was very still, then his arms came around her, enfolding her like a refuge against the storm. He said nothing, letting her give vent to her distress, his thumb lightly stroking the silky curls at the nape of her neck.

After a while the worst of her panic subsided, her

sniffles died away, and she gulped and rubbed the tips of her fingers over her wet cheeks.

'I'm s—sorry,' she mumbled chokingly into his shirt; 'now I've made you soggy. I don't usually go to pieces like this.' She dabbed ineffectually at the fine material.

'It's all right, Lissa. Calm down. Whatever it is, it can be sorted out.'

His voice was gravelly, deep, sure. . .and distinctly not what she had been expecting.

'A—Adam?' she faltered, clumsily pushing the damp tendrils of hair from her face, as she slowly lifted her head to look up at him.

This was not real, she told herself faintly. She was hallucinating. The shock of the broken glass and the letter had sent a fever through her brain, so that her mind was playing devilish tricks on her. That was the answer. There was no way this could really be happening. She couldn't possibly have let herself get tangled up in the arms of Rourke Deveraugh, not in her wildest dreams.

'Wrong man,' Rourke said tersely, his mouth taking on a grim slant. 'Lover-boy is engaged elsewhere. You'll have to make do with me.'

CHAPTER FOUR

LISSA stared up at him in dazed confusion. 'But why are you here? I thought——'

'I should refrain from attempts to exercise your brain if I were you,' he advised her tautly. 'It obviously doesn't agree with you.'

She glowered, her green eyes fierce with resentment. 'A few sweeteners wouldn't go amiss on your acid tongue,' she muttered.

'Really? And what happened to yours, might I ask? Judging from your usual acerbic frame of mind, I imagine you flushed them down the sink long ago.'

'That's exactly the kind of sneering remark I might have expected from you,' she observed in an aggrieved tone. 'It's no wonder we're always at odds with each other. You're high-handed and bigoted and contemptuous of everything I do. Well, let me tell you, the feeling's mutual. In fact, I think I hate you.'

'Feel free,' he said. 'It's a strong, powerful emotion. At least if you're directing that towards me it shows you know who I am.' His lips twisted into a cold smile. 'Discriminating between men is evidently not your strong point. Perhaps a few lessons might be in order.'

'What do you mean by that?' She viewed him with deep suspicion, all too conscious of the threat under-

lying his words. He was ruthless, arrogant, a man
who casually did just as he pleased and to hell with
the consequences, and it dawned on her that she was
in dangerously close proximity to him. She tried a
step backwards, testing the ground, and his hands
tightened on her arms, gripping her shoulders.

'I mean,' he said harshly, 'that I haven't finished
with you yet.' His eyes glittered like steel in the
moonlight, and she felt her skin burn beneath the
imprisoning band of his fingers. 'It's clear that you're
finding the strain of an illicit relationship hard going.
I'd like to think that it was remorse that made you
come sobbing into Adam's arms that way, but I'm
not so naïve as to believe it. You came out here to
whimper over the fact that you couldn't be together
in the way that you would like, only you made the
unfortunate mistake of running into me instead.'

'It isn't true,' she denied vehemently, 'it wasn't
that way at all; it was just——' She broke off.

'Just what?' His brow rose in insolent query. 'A
pact of mutual commiseration? Spare me, please.'

'No, you're wrong. . .' Her voice trailed away
again. How could she tell him about that dreadful
note, about what had really driven her out here? He
would want to know the ins and outs of it, to seek
out the deep dark passages of her mind, the intricacies of her life as it had been before. She did not
know herself what lay behind the cryptic words, and,
whatever it was, he would decide she was to blame
for anything that befell. She could do without his
censure.

'It has nothing to do with you anyway,' she said crossly. 'Mind your own business.'

'Good advice,' he said. 'I think I'll take you up on it. After all, you confused me with someone else, and I really shouldn't care for you to make the same mistake twice. Maybe a little reminder will help to fix me in your memory.'

Reading a dark and devilish intent in his grim expression, she made a sudden frantic attempt to twist free from his grasp; but she was too late. His movements were far too quick and self-assured for her efforts to succeed. Her eyes widened, and she swallowed down her growing panic, as with cool deliberation he pushed her back against the tree.

She said hoarsely, 'This is crazy; you can't do this. . .'

'Can't I?' he said grittily, closing in on her, using the pressure of his long body to pinion her there. 'Stop me, then, why don't you?'

Her senses reeled as the softness of her curves made an incandescent fusion with his hard male strength, her mind registering shock at the heated intimacy of the contact. She had stopped breathing. She could not move. All her consciousness was centred on that unfamiliar and earth-shattering friction.

His palm slid between her spine and the bark of the tree. 'See how thoughtful I am?' he muttered thickly. 'No bruises to complain of this time.' His other hand flattened against the trunk at the side of her head and he stared down at her, his eyes brilliant with the anger sparking in their depths, his mouth firm, only inches away from her own.

She tried to speak, but her throat was dry and no words would come. Her ears buzzed, the dizzying pulse of her blood hammering at her temples, and then any thought in her head that she might escape, even at this late stage, fragmented in an explosion of heart-stopping sensuality as he bent his head and took her mouth with his own. It was a fierce, possessive kiss, filled with burning demand, a determined, insistent plundering of her mouth that sent a hectic spiral of heat to curl along her nerve-endings. He shifted slightly, the hard thrust of his hips angled into hers, and a shameful excitement rippled through her body, a swift, unbidden flame of desire throbbing into every crevice of her being.

After a while, that first storm of angry passion seemed to dissolve, and his lips began a probing exploration, his hand shaping the length of her body and coming to rest warmly on the rounded curve of her hip. Weakness invaded her as his tongue darted over the fullness of her soft lips, dipped to taste the sweet moistness within. A mumbled, incoherent sound bubbled and surfaced in her throat, and she clung to him for support, her fingers twisting in the silk of his shirt.

Lissa felt the heavy thudding of his heart beneath her fingers, and knew that his actions had gone beyond anger, beyond a need purely to dominate. Now he was driven by a sensual hunger, a desire to satisfy a deep and powerful instinct that she had no strength, no will to fight. The ease with which he had provoked her own tumultuous response alarmed her. How could he have such an effect on her? Surely she had some defence against the tantalising assault he was wreaking on her senses? Desperately, she tried to break away, and he lifted his head, and stared down at her, his breathing thick and laboured.

'Now will you remember who I am?' he muttered harshly. 'I'm Rourke—is that clear, have you got that?'

She said thickly, 'I don't need any prompting to recall your name. It goes along with manhandling and arrogance and sheer male chauvinism.'

'I believe you said that before. At least now we've established something. Next time you rush into my arms you won't have any trouble distinguishing me from my partner.'

'Next time?' Her voice rose on a note of hysteria. 'Don't kid yourself.' Tearing herself away from him, she viewed him distractedly, her mouth still sweetly aching from the impact of his kisses. 'There isn't going to be a next time.'

'I wouldn't be too sure about that, if I were you.' His glinting eyes mocked her, and a tremor of some indefinable emotion wafted through her and raised all the fine hairs on her skin.

'One of these days,' she pointed out shakily, 'you'll get your come-uppance and I shall be first on the scene to applaud.' Slowly she chafed her arms with her fingers, aware now of the coolness of the late evening.

He laughed. 'You'll probably get tired of waiting.' Moving away from her a little, he flexed his shoulder muscles, stretched, and looked around. 'I came out here for a breath of air,' he said, 'but I guess it's time to go back now. There's a breeze springing up over the lake. Come on, I'll walk you to the house.'

'I'm not going back,' she said, standing her ground.

'It's cool out here,' he murmured. 'You don't have a jacket.'

'It doesn't matter; I don't want to go back yet.'

His eyes narrowed. 'Are you still expecting Adam to join you?' he enquired, an edge of frost creeping into his tone.

'Adam was never going to join me,' she retorted. 'I want to stay out here, that's all, and I would much prefer to be alone.' She sent him a taut scowl.

His mouth twisted. 'Do you have to be so perverse all the time? It doesn't make any sense, when you're obviously feeling chilled.'

'It's a condition known as shock,' she informed him tightly. 'An aftermath of the way you mauled me. I don't want to go in and have anyone see me. How can I face people when I must look as if I've just gone ten rounds with an all-in wrestler?' Tentatively she tested her tender and swollen lips with the tip of her tongue.

'You're prone to exaggeration too, I see.' His voice was amused. 'You look fine, and anyway, if you don't want to see anyone you can go through the annexe. It's completely private. I'll show you.' He put out a hand to her and she slapped it away.

She didn't want him to touch her. It was too unsettling, made her feel too hot and bothered. It wasn't fair that he could make her senses rocket in such a devastating way.

'And how am I to explain my abrupt disappearance to my host? she asked tersely. 'He may not be your favourite person at the moment, but Adam did invite me and it is his home that I would be wandering about in.'

He studied her broodingly. 'Actually, you're wrong. Adam may have extended the invitation, but it happens to be my house.'

She stared at him. 'Yours?' Her jaw dropped, her lips parting in disbelief.

'Mine.' He reached out a finger and tilted it under her chin, closing her mouth. 'I've no objection which part of it you want to explore, but I could strongly recommend the bedroom. Delicate shades of blue, and an invitingly large double bed. Very soft, very comfortable.'

Lissa gave a distracted yelp and jumped away from him, wide-eyed with horror.

He grinned. 'That, I take it, was a negative answer?'

She gave him a fulminating glare. 'This is not funny. I can't think why you have to constantly provoke me this way.'

'You make such an easy target,' he drawled. 'How could I possibly resist?'

He turned away from her and began to walk in the direction of the house, and after a moment's hesitation she followed. Why was this man such an enigma? Why was it that he could succeed in getting under her skin this way? It wasn't fair.

The annexe was a small extended wing round the back of the house. Rourke unlocked an oak-panelled door, flicking on a switch as he entered, flooding the room with light. A workroom of some sort, she noted fleetingly, going in after him.

'You never tell me the truth,' she said in annoyance. 'You're always keeping something back.'

'You didn't ask,' he returned moderately. 'What do you want to know? The sheets are silk—cool for the spring, I don't wear——'

'Stop,' she wailed, covering her ears in a childlike gesture. 'I don't want to know. Why are you still tormenting me? You know perfectly well what I meant.'

'Do I?' he said, his blue eyes gleaming with light mockery. 'I could hazard a guess, I suppose.' His glance slanted over her. 'What a strange mixture you are, Lissa. An intriguing combination of innocence and sensuality.'

'Don't keep changing the subject,' she complained in frustration. 'You're an infuriating man, Rourke Deveraugh. I don't know why I let you annoy me this way.'

'You're just crotchety because you enjoyed my kissing you and you can't come to terms with it,' he said mildly.

Colour flared in her cheeks. 'That is not true,' she denied hotly. 'I'm angry because—because you think you can add me to a long line of women notched on your belt. It feeds your ego to flirt with me, doesn't it? That way you can tell yourself you took me from another man.' She sucked in a breath. 'And that's another thing,' she went on, rousing herself to a pitch of indignation. 'You set yourself up as judge and jury, and yet who are you to decide matters—a man who spent the evening philandering with his secretary!'

'Not the whole evening, Lissa,' he rebuked her softly, and her already pink cheeks grew even warmer. He looked at her with interest. 'Does my. . . involvement. . .with my secretary bother you?'

'Not—not at all,' she denied swiftly, a catch in her voice. 'You do whatever you please with whoever, as long as you keep away from me. I was merely surprised to note that someone who professes to take such a high moral stance should be cavorting freely with a married woman. She does wear a wedding-ring, I noticed.'

He said evenly, 'Rebecca divorced her husband a couple of years ago. There's no reason for her to remove her ring. Besides, I think she feels it gives her status, and protection.'

'But not from you, evidently,' Lissa shot back.

Rourke grinned faintly. 'What can all this hot air be covering, I wonder? If it isn't to do with your feelings about me, what other issue can you be trying to evade? Of course, you did make it clear that I hadn't disturbed a lovers' tryst out there by the lake, so I'm curious to know what did send you rushing through the grounds in such a state of agitation?'

Her brow furrowed. She had forgotten that slip she had made; she might have known that he would pick her up on it sooner or later. He was far too perceptive. She would have to be more careful, keep a better hold on her tongue.

'A fit of the blues,' she said with some diffidence. 'It happens every now and again. There doesn't have to be a particular reason.'

'I doubt that,' he said, casting a speculative glance over her. 'Something was bothering you the first time we met, and you kept quiet about that, too. It could have been Adam on your mind, I suppose, but I'm beginning to think that there's a little more to it than that.'

'Since it has nothing whatever to do with you, I'd appreciate it if you would just forget the whole thing,' she retorted.

'I'm sure you would.' His mouth made a brief, humourless smile. 'You're a lady of mystery, full of secrets waiting to be unlocked, but that's no problem. I'll find the key eventually. It's only a matter of time.'

His calm certainty unnerved her. 'Why bother?' she asked, thankful that her voice remained steady.

His gaze was deep, unwavering. 'Mysteries have always intrigued me,' he said.

Lissa turned away from his cool scrutiny. Looking around the room, she saw that it was, indeed, a workroom. Not as clearly defined as the one back at his office, more like a study really, with a desk and filing cabinet, a bookcase against one wall, and beneath a wide window a long, narrow work-top cluttered with various pieces of gadgetry. She moved towards it to take a better look, glad of the chance to withdraw a little from his disturbing presence.

There was an assortment of equipment, some of

which she recognised; others she was not too sure about. An electronic keyboard linked to a printer caught her attention, and she studied it, frowning thoughtfully.

'Isn't this an amplifier of some kind?' she asked, examining the interface with care. 'I didn't know Lynx dealt with this sort of thing.'

'We don't usually. It's something I'm working on, developing out of my own interest.'

'Show me,' she demanded. 'Show me how it works.'

'You have to put these on first,' he said, indicating a pair of headphones.

Lissa did as she was told, and obligingly he tapped out a few words on the keyboard. There was a momentary pause, and then the sentence he had typed was repeated in soft tones through the right-hand earpiece. She blinked, startled, then slowly replaced the headset on the table.

'It's meant to be operated by the blind,' he explained. 'It's linked in with an audio tape facility which comes through the left earpiece, and the computer sound connects with the other.'

Her eyes widened. 'You designed this?'

He nodded absently, his attention absorbed by the print-out.

Her glance roamed the work-top. 'And this one?' She indicated another keypad, connected to a contraption made up of levers and pulleys.

'Oh, that's just a model.' He pressed a button on the pad, which brought into play several highly synchronised movements. 'The real thing's much bigger. Hopefully, it'll give some severely disabled people a means of getting out of the bath without having to rely on another person.'

Lissa shook her head in amazement, spreading her palm in a gesture to encompass the equipment. 'But these are fantastic. Why aren't you marketing them?'

'They still need one or two modificatons.'

'But they work perfectly.'

'Not as perfectly as they could.'

She stared at him in wondering exasperation. The man had a couple of world-stoppers on his hands and he wasn't ready to part with them. He was biding his time, thinking up even more facilities to add, when what he had created was magnificent already. The mind that had conjured up those designs had to be brilliant—annoying, devious, prone to flights of fancy—but brilliant all the same.

She said, 'You do realise that these designs could be worth thousands of pounds, don't you?'

He shrugged. 'Maybe. Money isn't the issue. I'm comfortable as I am, and Lynx is well ahead of its competitors. I don't see any need to rush into things.'

Lissa rolled her eyes. How many layers were there to this man? Her assessment of him was forever being turned on its head. Each time she thought she had caught hold of the essential man he turned out to be as nebulous as the sea mist drifting through her fingers. Neptune was clearly working overtime with this particular denizen of the deep.

'I think there's every reason to get them out as quickly as possible,' she persisted. 'You shouldn't be sitting on a breakthrough as big as this.'

'Since you're not involved in the project,' he muttered tersely, 'it needn't be of any concern to you.'

She took his put-down without rancour, allowing her gaze to drift over the paperwork scattered in separate clumps of disorder at intervals along the work-bench. 'Shouldn't this all be filed away?' she asked, waving a hand over the nearest pile. 'If you had this lot in order, it might help to get you to the production stage a bit quicker.'

'You might enjoy that kind of thing,' he said with more than a touch of irritation, 'but I have other matters to see to, more important than shifting a few papers about.'

She lifted a brow. 'Are you suggesting that I should do it for you?' she queried sweetly.

His teeth met. 'I don't need you to interfere,' he grated. 'I know exactly where everything is. I can manage quite well without anyone poking around in here.'

She cast a glance over the assortment of coffee-mugs littering the surface, and sniffed disparagingly. 'I should think a dishwasher would come in handy. Don't you ever wash out your coffee-cups?'

He gave her an abstracted look. 'I forget. It's easier to fetch out a clean one, and have a marathon plunge at the end of the week.'

Her nose wrinkled in distaste. 'I can imagine you would think that way.' She made a brief mental count of the crockery. 'From the looks of things, you're addicted to the stuff.'

'It keeps me alert,' he said. 'Helps me to think better.'

'There are other ways,' she told him with Spartan vigour. 'Like jogging, or taking a brisk swim. You'd be fitter, too.' Not that his tautly muscled frame showed any sign of laxity, she admitted in silent acknowledgement. The man was primed, like an athlete.

'Is that what you do? he questioned musingly. 'Indulge in a work-out each morning?' He appraised her slowly, then nodded, as though making up his mind. 'We could always try it together, I suppose. The idea does conjure up some interesting connotations.'

Lissa's breath hissed through her teeth. 'Back off, Rourke. I've no intention of participating in any kind of sport with you.'

His mouth made a mocking smile. 'You disappoint me, Lissa. Are married men your only vice?'

She looked at him with brooding dislike. 'Dipping you in boiling oil could fast become another.'

Rourke bared his teeth, and in the tense moments that followed as they squared up to each other they heard the unmistakable sound of a cough, and turned to see Adam make an appearance in the doorway.

'Am I interrupting a fight?' he asked with interest. 'Any chance of a ringside seat?'

Rourke's growl was indecipherable to Lissa, but Adam seemed to take it in his stride. 'No?' he murmured. 'Maybe another time, then. Actually, Becky's been asking for you, Rourke. Seems you offered her a lift home, and she promised her baby-sitter she'd be back at a reasonable hour. Besides, you've monopolised Lissa long enough.' He grinned.

'She looks as though she could do with more agreeable company—such as myself.'

Lissa smiled wanly, and allowed Adam to reach for her hand and lead her out of the room. So she had been right about Rebecca after all, she thought as they walked back towards the main part of the house. Rourke was more to her than just an employer. How much more?

As they came nearer to the warmly lit lounge, the soft hum of conversation filtered over to her, and she heard the faint clink of a glass being replaced on a table. Her footsteps faltered. Memories of blood-red wine and cruelly glinting shards of glass came back to haunt her. It had been wickedly symbolic, stage-managed to stir in her a cold feeling of dread.

'What's the matter, Lissa?' Adam stopped walking and stared at her. 'You look very pale. Aren't you feeling well? You shouldn't let Rourke get to you, you know. His mood swings are generally only related to the latest project he's working on. He doesn't mean anything by it—it just so happens that he inflicts his pent-up frustrations on the person nearest to hand. In this case—you.'

She shook her head. 'It isn't that. Perhaps I'm just tired. It's been a long day—I spent hours working on a new program. I'll probably feel better after a good night's sleep.' She frowned, trying to dislodge the piercing finger of doubt that stabbed inside her head. How safe would she be in her own flat, if some crazed person was determined to hunt her down? She shivered, and Adam draped an arm around her shoulders.

'You've probably been working too hard,' he said, giving her a penetrating stare. 'What you need is a weekend off, a complete break from anything to do with computers and logistics.' He thought for a moment, then added. 'Of course, why didn't I think of it before? I've a small cottage down by the coast—it isn't being used this weekend. Why not drive down there and enjoy a couple of days of sun and sea?' He paused. 'Well, perhaps not sun, if the weather forecast's anything to go by—but at least it would be a change of scene for you.'

She debated the idea for a while. It might well give her a better perspective on things if she could get right away for a short time. She'd be able to think more clearly if she was away from Eastlake, and perhaps come up with the answer as to who was behind these menacing notes.

'Are you sure it's all right?' she asked. 'What about Emma? What if she decides she would like to go to the cottage?'

'She won't,' Adam said with confidence. 'Don't worry about that. Emma has arranged to spend the weekend with a cousin, so there's no possibility of being disturbed. Just pack your bags and load up the car, and leave all the other arrangements to me. I can phone through and make sure that there'll be enough groceries to last through till Monday.'

She nodded slowly. 'I think I'd like that,' she said.

Rourke's gravel-timbred voice cut across the cool night air. 'Planning a weekend away, Lissa?'

She jumped at the unexpected intrusion. Adam said, 'I haven't been down to the cottage in an age. It always makes me feel good. It must be the change in air down there.'

'Is that where you're going?' Rourke asked.

'That's right,' Lissa answered, her tone crisp. 'Any objections?'

'None at all. It may do wonders for your temperament.'

'I'm sure it will,' she murmured. 'Being away from you is bound to have a positive effect.'

Rourke's smile was cynical. 'What a pity I have to be at the Brooksby plant this weekend,' he said. 'A trip to the coast sounds a much more inviting prospect.' Walking past her, his stride long and rangy, he went on into the house.

'Heaven forbid,' Lissa shuddered.

'I think,' Adam said with a grin, 'you and he have a few problems to sort out.'

The skies had darkened ominously as she set out on her journey to the coast, but she was not unduly concerned about the dismal weather. Even when lightning lit the skies and the floodgates opened when she was still twenty miles from her destination she merely flicked on the car's wipers and peered out into the black night, letting the piercing beam of the headlights guide her along the road. Adam had warned her that one stretch near to the coast had a dubious reputation for flooding, but she did not let that worry her. Surely, she mused, it hadn't been raining long enough for the water levels to rise that far, and even though the middle of the week had proved consistently wet she felt confident she would arrive at the cottage long before the possibility became a reality. The MG was a seasoned trooper, steadily eating up the distance, and it left her thoughts free to wander where they chose.

It was too dark to see much of the cottage when she did finally arrive, and, in any case, getting soaked as she lifted her belongings out of the boot did not encourage her to spend time looking around. Quickly she locked up the car. There was a small garden in front of the house, and she hurried along the crazy-paving path which led up to the gabled front porch.

Dropping her bags down on the hall floor, she gave a sigh of relief as she shook the raindrops from her hair, and eased her thin jacket from her shoulders. Hooking it over a conveniently placed rack, she walked through to the sitting-room.

Two lamps glowed softly from brackets on the wall, and she stared at them stupidly, her thoughts unfocused, her mind disorientated. Her gaze drifted, hazed, and then fastened with stark clarity on the man who unfurled his long limbs from the deep-cushioned armchair and rose to greet her.

'Hello, Lissa,' Rourke said. 'Did you have a good journey?'

CHAPTER FIVE

Lissa's pulse leapt like the rising hackles of an angry cat. 'I thought this place was empty,' she hissed. 'Why have you turned up again like the bad penny?'

'I can see that my presence must have come as something of a shock,' he said. 'I apologise for that.' The blue eyes glinted, his jaw was firm, strong. He did not look the least bit sorry, Lissa decided irritably.

The slow burn of resentment smouldered inside her. Why was it that he had this profoundly unsettling effect on her? Whenever he was around, her whole metabolism jerked into overdrive. What was it about him that constantly stirred her into such a state of agitation?

She viewed him mutinously. He stood there, long, lean and totally without concern, the clothes he wore only serving to emphasise the dark arrogance of the man. Black jeans encased his tautly muscled legs, a black sweater outlined the breadth of his shoulders and drew her eyes down to the firmly tapering waist.

Without haste he began to move towards her, and she stiffened. She hated that demonic air of self-assurance that went with him. He was a superbly male animal, he was used to beguiling women with his dark sorcery, but she would not be counted among them. She would not allow herself to be pulled inexorably towards some unknown destiny that he had in mind. He was dangerous to her, a predator who threatened her nervous system merely by being in the same room.

'Why aren't you at the Brooksby plant?' she demanded to know. He had done this to annoy her; that was the truth of the matter. He was determined to torment her in any way he could.

'I found that my presence there wasn't necessary after all,' he said smoothly. 'Wasn't that fortunate?'

'You mean that you changed your mind again, so that you could be sure to provoke me,' she snapped. 'It seems to be a tedious habit of yours.'

He smiled, and she saw the gleam of perfect white teeth. The effect on her temper was mercurial, but he was not going to succeed in getting to her, she decided. Whatever scheme his devious brain was concocting was doomed to failure.

'You've no business being here,' she informed him with razor-edged control. 'I suggest you leave, right now.'

'You want me out of the way before Adam arrives. No wonder you look a little distracted,' he murmured coolly. 'A threesome was not quite what you had in mind, was it?'

'Get out, Deveraugh,' she snarled, 'and take your nasty insinuations with you.'

He folded his arms across his chest, his legs braced. 'And leave you alone here? In this isolated house, with the elements raging outside, and the windows rattling under the strain? Won't you be afraid while you sit down for your long wait?'

'No chance,' she declared firmly. 'I'm made of

sterner stuff than that. And I'll have my hatred of
you to keep my spirits surging in full force. Besides,
what makes you think I'm in for a long wait?'

'Inside information,' he said with smug satisfaction
that made her want to hit him. 'I suppose you would
have liked to drive down together, but of course he
had to deposit Emma at her cousin's house first, so
there was bound to be some delay.' He paused,
watching her closely. 'Unfortunately, something
came up—a trouble-shooting mission that required
Adam's special diplomatic talents—I'm afraid he's
going to be tied up for the major part of the weekend.
I do hope it isn't going to be too much of a disappointment for you.'

His obvious insincerity infuriated her. Her temperature rose ten points. 'You, I take it, had a hand
in setting up this mission? It wouldn't have occurred
to you to leave Adam in peace and let him have a
well-deserved weekend off, would it? But then, I
suppose it's a total fabrication, a complete sham, isn't
it?' Anger simmered inside her. 'Don't you think it's
time you stopped interfering in matters that don't
concern you?'

Rourke's gaze was cynical, but he said evenly
enough, 'You're upset. Well, of course, I knew that
you would be. Having your cosy liaison disrupted
was never going to go down easily, but think on the
bright side—at least I'm here to keep you company.
You won't have to be alone.'

Rage choked in her throat. 'Do you imagine, for
one moment, that I have any intention of spending
the weekend with a playboy like you—a philanderer

who drifts with the tide, takes opportunities where they come? Take yourself off, Mr Deveraugh—go play with the lightning, why don't you?'

He tutted softly. 'What a wild creature you are. Are you always this vengeful? Does it come naturally?'

'Only around you,' she fumed. 'You're the only one whose untimely end would give me intense pleasure. If you don't care to have me arrange it for you, why don't you remove yourself before it's too late?'

Her outburst left him unperturbed. 'What kind of a time are you going to have, stuck here inside these four walls with no one to take your mind off the pouring rain? There's going to be no let-up, you know. There won't be any fun in walking on the beach unless you enjoy doing battle with the storm. You ought to be thanking me for being so considerate.'

A scream of frustration strangled on her lips. 'Go back to Eastlake and concentrate on your own affairs. In fact, I have a brilliant notion—why don't you call on Rebecca? I'm sure *she'd* be more than happy to see you.'

'Rebecca's busy this weekend. I'm entirely at your disposal.'

She shuddered. 'Don't tempt me. Disposing of you is something I could dream about.' Her lips thinned in a forced smile. 'As you can see, you are not wanted here. I'm perfectly capable of organising my own activities without any input from you.'

He looked at her askance. 'Are you sure about

that? What about a game of chess—wouldn't that be more interesting than following a solitary pursuit— or how about gin rummy?' She did not bother to reply, her gaze withering him, and he went on thoughtfully, 'We could always get the Scrabble board out, I suppose. How's your vocabulary? No, don't tell me—arrogant, wasn't that what you said— and what was it? Bigoted? Chauvinistic?' He appeared to muse. 'You seem to have a fair enough command of the English language. I'm sure you'll manage just fine.'

Lissa ground her teeth. 'You're doing this on purpose,' she said tightly. 'You set up this whole thing deliberately, just to cause me the maximum amount of aggravation, didn't you? Well, let me tell you——'

'Ah, now I have it,' he said with a nod of satisfaction. 'You'd rather we spent the whole weekend fighting, wouldn't you?' He examined her features closely. 'Yes, I can see that you would. I can tell from the way you're sparking at me like a green-eyed cat that there's nothing you'd like more.' His glance wandered over her. 'What a feisty lady you are. I suppose there must be a warring side to your nature constantly bubbling away under the surface.' He shrugged negligently. 'That's OK, I can deal with it; I'm all for a good fight, especially with you as my opponent—it keeps life from being dull. Besides,' he added, his mouth making a devilish curve, 'I really do enjoy winning.'

'Please don't get immersed in another of your fantasies,' Lissa advised him tartly. Whether or not

FREE BOOKS CERTIFICATE

Mills & Boon

YES! Please send me my four **FREE** Best Sellers together with my **FREE** gifts. Please also reserve me a special Reader Service subscription. If I decide to subscribe, I shall receive four superb Best Sellers every other month for just £6.80 postage and packing free. If I decide not to subscribe I shall write to you within 10 days. Any **FREE** books and gifts will remain mine to keep. I understand that I am under no obligation whatsoever – I may cancel or suspend my subscription at any time simply by writing to you. *I am over 18 years of age.*

2A3B

MS/MRS/MISS/MR

ADDRESS

POSTCODE _____ SIGNATURE

POST TODAY
and we'll send you this cuddly Teddy Bear.

PLUS a free mystery gift!
we all love mysteries, so as well as the **FREE** books and cuddly Teddy, there's an intriguing mystery gift specially for you.

MILLS & BOON
FREEPOST
P.O. BOX 236
CROYDON
CR9 9EL

Pluto ruled her temperament, she would not rise to his bait. He was taking an unholy delight in her discomfiture and it was high time that he was taken down a peg. 'I've learned my lesson as far as you are concerned. Believe me, I've far better things to do than waste my breath arguing with you.'

'Now there's a sensible girl.' His voice was infuriatingly smooth. 'I knew you would see reason in the end. What's the point in our bickering, when we could simply relax and make the most of the situation?'

He walked over to a polished mahogany cabinet which appeared to house the stereo unit, and began to flick through a collection of LPs. 'What kind of music do you like?' he asked absently. 'Strauss? Brahms? Something else? A little music would make a nice accompaniment to our meal, don't you agree?' He picked out a record and studied the sleeve. 'Adam had the foresight to order in a good stock of food, I noticed. I'll have to sort out a suitable bottle of wine to go with it.'

'I am not about to sit down to a meal with you,' she said bitingly, 'Nor am I——'

'Oh, but you must be hungry after your long journey,' he insisted, putting down the record. 'And the least I can do, after the way your plans have been disrupted, is to try to make it up to you, in part— help you adapt a little more cheerfully to the circumstances.'

She savaged him with a vicious scowl. 'There is nothing,' she said caustically, 'that you could do that would make me in any way feel good.'

His mouth quirked wryly. 'Nothing? Are you quite sure about that? I seem to remember the other evening——'

'That was an aberration,' she cut in swiftly. 'As well you know. A few moments of complete mental instability when you were unscrupulous enough to take advantage of me. It certainly won't happen again.'

'Of course not,' he agreed, his tone utterly bland. 'I wouldn't dream of adding to your psychoses.' He eyed the hectic flush of her cheeks with interest. 'That wouldn't be playing by the rules, would it?'

'Are you going to leave?' she enquired with chilling dignity.

'I am not. Do you know, I find this place remarkably comfortable?'

One of these days, she told herself, she would find a way of spiking his guns once and for all. In the meantime, since she couldn't physically throw him out, she would find somewhere else to stay for the night. 'Then I'll take my leave of you,' she said tersely. 'You may ransack the larder and wine cellar to your heart's content. I'm sure I shall be much more comfortable in a hotel.'

He lifted a dark brow. 'Whatever makes you happy,' he said with a mocking inflexion. 'Run away, if you must, if the thought of spending the night here with me is causing you so many qualms. You're obviously not as self-assured as you lead people to believe. I think,' he added obligingly, 'you'll find the nearest hotel is five or six miles down the main road. This does tend to be rather an out-of-the-way place,

I'm afraid. Pleasant if you're looking for peace and quiet, but it does have its drawbacks.'

She smiled briefly. 'Thank you so much for the information,' she muttered with cold politeness. 'I'm sure I'll find it. Do have a nice weekend.'

Outside, the rain was coming down in drenching sheets, and she huddled into her jacket against the driving wind as she hurried to the car. What sort of weather was this? As if she didn't have enough troubles to contend with. Rourke had set up the whole annoying episode. As usual, he thought he could do just as he pleased, without any regard for the consequences. It was altogether too much. Why did she have to keep crossing swords with that fiendish man?

Sliding into the driver's seat, she slammed the door shut and turned her key in the ignition. The engine fired and she pushed her foot down on the accelerator so that the fierce roar echoed her feelings of pent-up frustration. She scowled. He wasn't going to get away with it. If he thought he could manipulate her, he'd soon find out that it was a wasted effort. His journey had been completely unnecessary. Anyway, what was this obsession he had with her and Adam? Why was he constantly jumping to conclusions? Nothing she said made any difference. He thought he knew it all, and that was where he was going to come unstuck. Just wait till she saw Adam again. She'd get this thing sorted out.

She peered out through the windscreen into the eerie blackness of the winding lane. Rain hissed against the tyres, and the beat of the wipers became almost hypnotic. How much further would it be before she reached the main road? If only she'd paid more attention on the way down here. Her nerves were shot to pieces, that was the trouble. With one thing and another, she needed a break from all this hassle.

Where was the turn-off? Surely it must be here somewhere? The car's headlights picked out a road sign and she swung slowly left on to the narrow lane indicated. It couldn't be far now, a couple of miles perhaps. Another sign loomed ahead and she frowned into the darkness, slowing up as she approached it.

The sinking feeling came on her suddenly, lying like a leaden weight in her stomach as her eyes scanned the wording. Floods. She might have guessed. Wasn't that just the typical end to a perfectly awful day?

Drawing the car to a halt by a grass verge, she slumped dejectedly over the wheel, resting her head on her hands. Now what was she going to do? It seemed that everything was conspiring against her. She couldn't go on any further, and finding an alternative route in this black, rainswept landscape was not going to be an easy task. Besides, Adam had said it was a long detour to get back on to the main road, if this lane was cut off.

Lifting her head, she gazed around bleakly, and sighed. No wonder Rouke had made no move to stop her. He must have known all along that she would run into this set-back. Drumming her fingers on the wheel, she contemplated her options. The prospect of spending the night in the car was not a welcome one. The rain had succeeded in filtering through her thin jacket to the blouse beneath, and in her present damp state she'd probably finish up with pneumonia or some such ailment.

The only other alternative was to go back to the cottage, as well he'd known. Grimacing, she turned the key in the ignition once more, and brought the car around the way she had come. Wretched man. If she caught a cold through all this dreary journeying it would be all his fault. Serve him right if she sneezed all over him.

He was lounging on the sofa when she returned to the house, his long legs propped up on a low onyx table, while he flicked his way desultorily through the pages of a paperback.

'If you knew,' she said, pithily, as she marched into the room, 'and I'm sure you did, judging from your smug expression, why didn't you tell me?'

'Would you have believed me? Even if I'd told you that I heard it on the local news, I doubt you'd have taken my word for it. Knowing you, you'd have shot off anyway.' He shrugged, tossing the book on to the table and swinging his legs down to the floor. 'The road's usually clear until the river floods its banks. I thought it just as well to let you find out for yourself.'

'Wasn't that good of you?' she remarked through stiff lips. 'Thanks to you, I'm soaked to the skin.' Taking off her jacket, she dropped it over the back of a chair and picked distastefully at the damp folds of her burgundy skirt.

He stood up. 'Then come over to the fire and steam a little.'

She was tempted to ignore any suggestion that he made, but the orange flames that flickered in the grate looked invitingly warm, and it was more than she could do to stay away. Brushing the unruly wet tendrils of hair from her cheeks, she went over to stand in front of it, holding out her hands to the heat.

'It wouldn't have hurt you,' she said bitterly, 'to have done the gentlemanly thing and got out of here earlier, before the flood started.'

'Why should I leave my own house?'

She stared at him in shock. 'Yours? But Adam said——'

'We share the use of it,' he answered casually, and her teeth clamped.

'I suppose,' she muttered, 'that the fishing hut by the lake belonged to you as well.' She paused. 'Though I fail to see why you had to break the door down.'

'Forgot my key,' he said drily.

Her mouth twisted. 'It's a pity you didn't forget the key to this place,' she told him. 'I don't see why I shouldn't enjoy a little privacy, since Adam invited me.'

He sent a brooding frown in her direction. 'I prefer to keep an eye on what's going on.'

'Nothing's going on,' she said, honing her words to a steel edge. 'Haven't I told you that often enough?'

'So you have, but my sister seems to think otherwise.'

Lissa stared at him, a frown pulling at her brow. 'Your sister? You'll have to explain. . . I don't understand.'

'Adam's wife,' he said tersely. 'We're talking about Emma, who happens also to be my sister.' His blue eyes glittered harshly as he challenged her gaze. 'For that reason, if for no other, I'm going to do all that I can to make sure that your sordid little affair doesn't succeed. I've no intention of standing by and watching Emma get hurt because of a deadly man-trap like you.'

Lissa gasped. His words hurt her more deeply than she would have imagined. What kind of person did he think she was? Did he seriously believe that she had set out to break up a woman's marriage? It was untenable that he should blame her for something that was not her fault.

She said angrily, 'How do you know that Emma suspects me of being the root cause of her troubles? Perhaps she was just feeling generally unhappy, and you put two and two together and made five. I don't see why you should assume I have anything to do with it.'

'I'm going on what she told me,' he rasped. 'Isn't it obvious why she points the finger at you? There was a time when you and Adam were more than friends——'

She opened her mouth to deny it, and he cut her off. 'And these days you're always together, she hardly ever sees him any more——'

'Only because he works so hard,' Lissa broke in. 'Why do their difficulties have to involve me? Why am I cast as the scarlet woman all the time?'

His lips twisted in scorn, and Lissa hated him for that look. 'Their problems have nothing to do with me. Your sister should look somewhere else for the answer, then maybe she'll begin to sort things out. For a start, she ought to be talking to Adam, not spilling out her troubles to you.'

'Perhaps she did, and when she came up against a brick wall she turned to me. Our parents live some distance away, she only gets to see them every few weeks, but I'm close to hand, I'm here to listen. She's always confided in me, trusted me to help.'

'I hardly see you in the role of agony aunt,' Lissa said tightly. He assumed she was guilty, took it for granted that she was at the foot of everything, and that left a bitter taste in her mouth.

'What do you expect me to do?' he queried, looking at her with dislike. 'She might be a grown woman, but deep down she's still my baby sister, and she's hurting badly. Would you have me turn her away?'

Lissa expelled her breath slowly. No, of course he couldn't do that. It was only her own hyped-up state that made her goad him. He was bound to try to help Emma, wasn't he? His own innate Jupiterian integrity would see to that.

'I'm sorry,' she said flatly. 'Of course, you're right. But I still think you should try allowing some credibility on my side too.'

'Should I? And where does this cosy little arrangement with Adam fit into that scenario, this convenient weekend away?'

'It doesn't,' she said, suddenly very weary. 'There never was any arrangement of that kind, but I don't expect you to take my word for it. That would be too much to hope for.' Her gaze clouded. 'I came here to be on my own to have a chance to think something through. My only involvement with Adam is through a business deal.'

He viewed her with scepticism, and she turned away from him, heavy with the knowledge that he would never believe her, and too tired to keep up the argument. Absently, she rubbed at her arms to keep away the chill that swept over her.

'You'd better get out of those wet things,' he said curtly.

Her jaw firmed. 'I'll decide what I need to do,' she gritted, then studiously ignored him.

'Please yourself,' he murmured. 'Just don't collapse on me, will you? It's difficult enough dealing with you when you're halfway normal—I dread to think what you might be like in a state of delirium.' His blue glance slanted over her. 'Besides,' he went on, 'I've no objection to your dripping all over the carpet. Wet's a condition that suits you.'

The clinging nature of her garments was borne in on her with horrifying clarity as her startled gaze caught the back end of his grin. She gave a smothered yelp of dismay.

The man was a monster. 'I'm going to bed,' she muttered, averting her face so that he would not see the heated flush that stained her cheeks. She plucked her jacket from the chair. 'Is there a shower or bath I could use?'

'Upstairs, first door on your left.' There was amusement in his tone. 'I think you're very wise. A warm shower might do wonders for your nerves.'

Fiend. She steeled herself to remain calm in the face of his baiting. Her glance flickered in his direction. 'And which room is to be mine?'

She could almost see the baring of his shark's teeth. Heaven forbid that she should wander into any of his territorial waters. She had the feeling he would swallow her whole if she so much as rippled the surface. Tomorrow, when she'd had a good night's sleep, she'd be much better capable of dealing with him. Tonight she was over-wrought, ragged from the tribulations of the day, and there was no way she could cope with any more of his side-swipes. The morning would give her a different perspective on things. She hoped.

'Second on the right. I'm sure you'll find it comfortable, but if there's anything you need in the night do let me know. I'll do my best to oblige.'

She looked at him sharply, but it was impossible to read anything in his enigmatic expression. 'I'll manage,' she said, and made a strategic withdrawal, picking up her case from the hall as she went.

Emerging from the fragrant warmth of a sudsy bath some time later, Lissa dried herself carefully and slipped into a gold-coloured satin teddy. The water had helped to relax her a little, and the pale aquamarine hues of the bathroom had lent a soothing balm to her damaged spirits. Her room, too, was a pleasing

blend of cream and rose-pink, the colours of the
curtains picked out in the material of the plump
duvet and the matching bed linen. Everything had
been provided to make this room an attractive and
restful setting for any guest. On the dresser, there
was a fluted crystal vase, filled with sprays of
beautifully scented freesias, and she went over to
sniff them appreciatively. Who could have put them
there?

Straightening, she reflected soberly that the only
thing missing was a lock on the bedroom door. Her
brows pulled together. Ought she to put a chair
under the handle? She dismissed the idea. Rourke
would not disturb her. He might be devious, but he
was not without principles.

Sliding between the bedcovers, she flicked off the
bedside lamp and snuggled down into the enveloping warmth. In the morning, with a clear head, she
would tackle all her problems. . .in the morning. . .
It was her last thought before she drifted into a deep,
satisfying sleep.

The duvet wound itself around her as she turned
and stretched in the big bed, her limbs languid with
heat. One arm disentangled itself from the covers,
her fingers curling indolently into the fine cotton of
the quilt. Snatches of dreams flitted through her head
and merged, one into another. A man, his familiar
image blurred by the sweet haze of sleep, called her
name softly, and she went to him, her face upturned
for his kiss, her lips soft and full, a smile lingering on
the pink contours of her mouth. But as she reached
him the vision shimmered and disappeared and she

was alone, stumbling as she tried to find her way through the shadows of a forest, mist cloaking the branches of the trees.

Her finger snagged on roughened bark, and she stared down at it, watching the bright droplets of blood trickle to the floor and settle among shards of broken glass. A whimper rose in her throat and hovered on her lips, and then she heard the man's voice, filtering through the layers of sleep. There was a fragrance too, a warm, tantalising aroma that wafted around and teased her nostrils. Slowly, she opened her eyes.

'Coffee,' Rourke said, placing a cup on the bedside table. 'It might help to wake you up.' He went over to the window and drew back the curtains to let in a grey, watery light, and she closed her eyes briefly against the muted glare.

'What time is it?' she muttered.

'Late,' he informed her. 'You've been sleeping for hours, so I thought you might be about ready to get up.'

She looked over to the window once more and heard the rain driving against the glass. 'It seems to me I'm in the right place,' she said. 'I think I might hibernate. Why don't you go away and leave me to it?'

'Feeling sorry for yourself, are you, since Adam isn't here to share your idyll?'

'Go away,' she said rudely, tugging the duvet to her chest, 'and take your baseless assumptions with you. I can do without your carping first thing.'

'Is burying yourself under the covers going to

provide the answer to your problems?' he asked
sceptically. 'I doubt very much that you'll get far that
way.'

'The door is over there,' she said pointedly. 'Why
don't you use it?'

He smiled. 'What a sweet girl you are. Drink your
coffee, Lissa,' he ordered. 'You'll feel like a new
person in two ticks.'

'I wish you would stop telling me what to do,' she
complained, reaching for the cup and sipping slowly.

He seated himself comfortably in a chair opposite
the bed, and hooked a footstool towards him with
the toe of his shoe.

She stared at him over the rim of her cup. 'Don't
you ever follow the rules of polite society?' she asked,
aggrieved. 'Could you not consider leaving the
room?'

'You might fall asleep again,' he said, picking up a
mug from the table beside him and taking a long
swallow. 'I'd rather we talked.'

She frowned. 'I've found that morning is not a
good time for conversation,' she murmured.

'On the contrary, it can be the very best. Perhaps,
to start with, you'd like to tell me why you felt that
you needed a bolt-hole? Assuming, of course, that
your story about Adam is the truth.'

Lissa stiffened. She sensed that Rourke could be a
man to rely on, a man whose strength would be a
bulwark against all odds, but he had always judged
her and found her wanting, and she was not ready
to let down her guard and confide in him. Where she
was concerned, he was too prone to condemn. What-

ever was behind the insidious threats she had received was something she had to work out for herself.

She said, lifting one naked shoulder dismissively, 'It isn't something I care to discuss. Especially not with you.'

'Then you can hardly expect me to show much appreciation of your view of things, can you?'

She did not answer. Putting down her cup, she reached for the silk robe laid out on a chair at the side of the bed. He thought he had the upper hand while she was trapped here, and he was right—it made her feel awkward and uneasy, put her at a disadvantage.

Slipping the garment over her naked shoulders, she pulled it around herself and fastened the belt. With the scarlet and gold robe firmly in place, at least she felt a little more in control of the situation. It was nerve-racking, having him watch her as she slid her feet out of bed, and pushed them into soft mules. He swallowed the last of the coffee and replaced his cup on the table.

'You drink too much of that,' she said, straightening, and allowing the fine drifts of material to swish to the floor.

'You sound like my mother. Being a nurse, she's always pointing out the dire effects of too much caffeine.'

'But you don't act on her warnings?'

He shrugged. 'I like it. It helps me to think.'

'It can't be helping much, if you keep coming up with crazy ideas about what I'm supposed to be up to.' She ran a hand fractiously through the bright tumble of her chestnut curls. 'Why are you so intent on believing the worst of me?'

He stood up, his deep blue glance moving over her in a slow appraisal that burned into the very pores of her skin, and she realised, in those few heart-stopping moments, what a mistake it had been to confront him. Dry-mouthed, she smoothed down the shimmering folds of her robe with fingers that shook slightly. He did not move, and yet it was as though he had reached out and touched her, the lick of his gaze like a flame spreading fever throughout every part of her.

'Why is it,' he returned thoughtfully, 'that whatever you do, however outrageous your behaviour, you still manage to cast your spell over me? You've the body of an angel holding out the lure of forbidden fruit, yet you're as insubstantial as a nymph who flits through the mountain streams. I put out a hand to grasp you, and you slip through my fingers like the quicksilver cascade of a waterfall. What chance do I have, what chance does any man have, once you start to weave your magic?'

He came closer, his hands curving around her arms, and she stared up at him, her eyes wide with uncertainty. He was the man from her dream; her own subconscious yearnings had surfaced in sleep, betrayed her, left her body in conflict with her mind. She was transfixed, unable to break away, her limbs weak, molten.

'What talisman is there,' he asked, his voice rough around the edges, 'that could protect me from you?

You rail at me, yet it has no effect. It only makes me want you all the more. It seduces me to kiss away the harsh words from your lips, to feel your mouth soften and tremble beneath mine.'

His thumbs stroked upwards over her arms, creating tiny whirlpools of warmth that permeated through the flimsy silk of her robe. He drew her against him, his lips seeking out the smooth plane of her cheek, the full, ripe curve of her mouth. The kiss was achingly sweet, a lingering delicious sensation that spun out in a timeless band of teasing exploration and honeyed conquest.

Where were her defences against this tender assault? What was the hold he exerted over her, that could steal beneath her guard and leave her so vulnerable to his own undeniable brand of charm? He folded her to him, coaxing her into the enchanted refuge of his arms, and she went willingly.

The outside world and all its adversities faded away to nothing in the heated thrill of his embrace. She had fought against him, tried to keep him out of her life, but wasn't that because she had been afraid? She had been hurt in the past, but that was over now. She was no longer a vulnerable young girl exposed with cruel suddenness to the harsh realities of life. Wasn't it time to put aside her fears and insecurities and give herself up to the heady delight of love and passion?

This man, out of all men, held the power to tantalise and entice, to bind her to himself. The dawning knowledge washed over her consciousness like waves breaking on a virgin shore. Was it possible? If only he believed in her, couldn't they together submerge themselves in the waters of Eden and be renewed for all time?

Rourke held her close, his hand tracing the slender column of her throat, his lips nuzzling the smooth pathway where his fingers led. Gently, he nudged aside the silken folds of her robe, and brushed his mouth over the creamy expanse of her flesh, his tongue dipping lightly to taste the shadowed valley between her breasts.

His hands stroked her, seeking out the rounded curve of hip and thigh, and her breath came raggedly, the beat of her pulse quickening with the increased urgency of his caresses. Slowly he pressured her backwards, tipping her on to the cushioning softness of the bed, moving over her so that the imprint of his body burned on her like a brand.

She shifted restlessly beneath him, her heart pounding out of control as she registered the powerful interplay of muscle and sinew. Her blood sang in her veins as his hands discovered her shapeliness, sought out the heavy fullness of her breast. His thumb slid over the swelling mound outlined beneath the silk, trailed over the ripening bud at its centre. She gasped, his name whispering over her lips as he stirred her senses and brought her temperature soaring to fever-pitch.

'Rourke. . .'

'I know, sweetheart. . . I know,' he muttered thickly. 'Stay with me, let me take you with me. I'll help you feel sensations you only ever dreamed of. You won't be sorry, I promise.'

She acknowledged his power over her. He made her feel incredibly feminine; the merest touch of his fingers transported her to ecstasies she had never before experienced. There was something about Rourke that stirred her in a way no other man had ever done. . .but, even so, a tiny voice of caution held her back. What did he feel for her? Was there anything more than desire in his quest of her?

Rourke seemed to sense her slight withdrawal from him. 'Forget about the past. Does anything of what's gone before really matter?' His voice dropped to a hoarse whisper. 'You don't need Adam. He's out of bounds, he'll never be able to make you happy, but you and I, Lissa, together we could reach the stars.'

He was still convinced of her guilt. Nothing she had said had changed his opinion of her. Unhappily, she averted her head so that he could not see the glimmer of tears that smarted behind her eyelids. How could she have forgotten what kind of man he was? The suspicion was always there; he only pursued her to quench an aching need. Rebecca was busy, he had said, so he had turned to Lissa. What chance was there that this man could ever love her or be faithful to one woman?

It had been a mistake to think that she could not be hurt again. This time, she knew, the pain would not disappear. It would always be there, through the years, a nagging sickness in the pit of her stomach.

She said huskily, 'Perhaps we could, but what is there afterwards? When you come back down to earth, is it on to pastures new? Why do men think that they can use women and come out of it unscathed?'

Rourke was silent for a moment, then he placed one arm on either side of her body and leaned over her. 'You have to forget him,' he said harshly. 'He was never yours in the first place. You know that, but you won't bring yourself to accept it.'

He pushed himself away from her and stood back from the bed, and the discordant ringing of the telephone shattered the silence of the room. His mouth tightened. 'Sooner or later,' he said, 'you'll have to let go, because I'll be right next to you to make sure of it.' Snatching up the phone, he growled into the mouthpiece.

Lissa drew her robe around herself in a protective gesture, her mind frozen over like a bleak winter landscape. How had it happened, this tragedy of falling in love with a man who could never be part of her destiny? Rourke Deveraugh had no interest in her other than a passing fancy. His greatest, his only concern was to ensure that she stayed away from his sister's husband.

Her gaze flickered as he replaced the receiver. 'What's wrong?' she asked, taking in the grey pallor of his face.

'Emma is in hospital,' he said woodenly. 'A threatened miscarriage.'

CHAPTER SIX

THERE was only one way that Lissa knew of to keep the demons of misery and desolation at bay. She would put all her energies into her work, and try to forge ahead regardless of the emotional upheaval that was erupting inside her.

The realisation of her feelings for Rourke had come as a shock, the more so because there was no chance he would ever come to care for her in return. He was an opportunist, who took advantage of the chances fate laid out for him, and this last weekend had been just such an example. It was a bitter irony that he condemned her for loving a man who was out of reach. How close he was to the truth, and yet how many light-years away. Rourke was the one who was shooting out of her sphere like a trail-blazing comet.

She was sifting desultorily through her work schedule when Adam rang her from the office. 'I need to take some things over to the hospital for Emma,' he said. 'Rourke is going to the Brooksby plant, and I'll be out for some time, so I wondered if you could come over and help Becky out with the computer? I know you have to come in anyway, to look at the disks for our new program.'

'Of course,' Lissa agreed, relieved that she would not have to endure a confrontation with Rourke while her emotions were still raw. 'Don't worry about it,' she said. 'I'll do whatever I can to help. Is Emma feeling any better?'

'She's stopped haemorrhaging now, and the doctors think they may be able to save the pregnancy—it's a question of making sure she rests completely.'

'She'll need your reassurance, Adam,' Lissa said quietly. 'Stay with her as much as they'll let you—don't worry about anything at the office—I'm sure Rourke will take care of whatever crops up.'

Although he agreed, it was obviously difficult for Adam to let go of the reins, as Lissa discovered when she arrived at Lynx some time later to find him still on the premises.

'Here's the key to the security cupboard where the confidential files are kept,' he told her. 'You'll need them for your programming. I forgot to mention that to Becky, but there won't be any problem. Anyway, you'll probably want to start with the normal day-to-day stuff—it's on disks that are kept in the cabinet. They're not locked up.'

'Is this the cupboard?'

He nodded, and Lissa opened it, then added the key to her own set and tossed them on to a ledge next to her bag. Gently, she coaxed him towards the door.

'Go to the hospital,' she said, resting a hand lightly on his arm. 'Stop worrying about things back here. I'm sure Becky can hold the fort—besides, I'll be around if I'm needed. You'll have to learn to delegate if you're going to be a father. Otherwise you'll suffer a burn-out before you're forty.'

'I know, you're right,' he sighed, giving her hand a gentle squeeze. 'Thanks for coming over.'

A thud sounded behind them, as Rourke kicked the door shut with the heel of his shoe. Lissa jumped, shocked to the core, and he scowled at her darkly. He was wearing a business suit, dark blue, finely striped, a waistcoat beneath the jacket lending austerity to his appearance. His shirt was crisp, the cuffs pristine. She took it all in, her heart thumping discordantly in her throat as she stared at him.

'You're here again, I see,' he said tersely. 'What's wrong? Couldn't you keep away? Perhaps you should take a course in self-denial.'

She sent him an answering glare, storm clouds gathering in the depths of her green eyes. 'Did I ever tell you that you're the most despicable man I ever met? I doubt even a lifetime's subscription to a class in good manners would do anything to improve your temperament.'

He ignored her, turning towards Adam. 'Shouldn't you be at the General?' he snarled.

Adam nodded, looking at them both oddly. 'I'm on my way. I've asked Lissa to keep an eye on the computer. It's been playing up again.'

'Really? It seems to me the thing can go back if it's going to give that much trouble. Then Lissa wouldn't need to be around so much, would she?'

Adam frowned. 'What's eating you, Rourke? If it's the problem over at Barton's, I can deal with it when I get back.'

'You'll do no such thing,' Rourke ground out impatiently. 'I'm going there myself when I've been to Brooksby. Get out of here, Adam, you're needed at the hospital.'

Adam did as he was told, making a hurried exit, and Rourke let his eyes skim coldly over Lissa. 'The computer is just an excuse,' he gritted. 'Don't think I'm not aware of that.'

'You think you know everything,' she answered tightly. 'One day you'll come down from your cold and lonely cloud and join the real world.'

Scorn edged his mouth. 'You're the one living in a fool's paradise,' he said. 'Take care your dreams don't turn to ashes in your mouth.'

He marched over to the workroom, and she watched him go, her throat painfully aching. It was not going to be easy, working here under the icy wash of Rourke's disapproval. She would get the job done as quickly as possible, and then leave. There would be no need for their paths to cross again.

She was hanging up the jacket of her plum-coloured suit when Rebecca came in through the outer door. Lissa greeted her, adding, 'If you have any hiccups with the new computer, just let me know. I'll do what I can to sort it out.'

The other woman nodded non-committally, and Lissa noticed that she looked pale and tense. Perhaps she was not feeling well, or it could be that she resented Lissa's intrusion into the office. Lissa was, after all, an outsider.

Hadn't Rourke made that all too plain? He did not want her here. Just the thought of having her around the place made him irritable. Did he think she would put his affair with Rebecca in jeopardy?

Frowning, she went over to the cabinet and selected a batch of disks. Rourke's hostility had unnerved her, and working with his girlfriend was not calculated to make her feel remotely cheerful.

Smoothing down her skirt as she seated herself, she reached over and started up the secondary computer. Why was he so angry with her? She had tried to explain about Adam, hadn't she? So why was he still venting his temper on her? He had wanted her, wanted someone—any woman would have served his need, she corrected herself sharply—and she had rejected him. That must be the thing that was plaguing him, riding him so hard. That, and the thought that the two women might clash. She looked up, tensing as he strode into the room.

'How long is that going to take?' he asked briskly.

Lissa hated the cold incisiveness of his tone, and she was angry with herself for caring so much. 'Two or three hours, maybe,' she said. She was a quick worker, and already last week she had made headway on Richard Blake's project, as well as starting work scheduled for one or two of her new contacts. 'I doubt that I'll disturb you for much longer.'

He came and stood behind her, staring over her shoulder at the screen, frowning darkly at the columns of figures displayed. How could he be so detached? she wondered feverishly. She found his nearness distracting. Her own thoughts wandered in chaotic disorder to recall the way his lips had taken possession of her own, the feel of his hands on her heated flesh.

He turned away and her mind jerked in confusion.

Rebecca was sifting restlessly through some of the papers in her in tray, and he went over to her.

'Are you feeling all right? You've no colour in your cheeks at all.' He put an arm around her shoulders, concern written on his face, and Lissa made an effort to quell the sharp stab of jealousy that tightened her stomach muscles. All *she* got from him was cold looks and icy dismissal.

'Do you think you should go home?' he asked.

'It's just a headache,' Rebecca said. 'I'll be fine in a while.'

'Hmm.' Rourke straightened. 'If you're sure. . . Take some aspirin, and lie down if you need to. Don't worry about those figures—I'll have a look at them later. Just see to the most urgent of the letters if you're up to it.'

Lissa kept her head down. He didn't care at all about any feelings *she* might have, she thought broodingly. Yet he would cosset Rebecca as if she were a tender plant that needed nurturing.

'I'll be out most of the morning,' he said quietly. 'You know where to reach me if you need to.'

Rebecca nodded, and he left the office, striding briskly to the car park.

Lissa heard the slam of his car door, and felt the knot inside her tighten. He had not said another word to her. He had dismissed her from his mind as he would swat away a troublesome fly. She had been right to be wary of any new involvement, to stop things before they went too far. His feelings had gone no deeper than the surface. Never again would she let herself be caught that way. From now on she would concentrate solely on work.

She spent the next hour jotting down notes as she processed each disk. The phone startled her when it rang, so engrossed was she, but Rebecca answered it, her voice quickly taking on a distracted note.

Lissa glanced across to the other woman. 'Is there anything I can do?' she asked, as Rebecca put the receiver down.

Rebecca worried at her lip. 'I have to go out. Adam wants me to collect some things that he forgot, and take them to the hospital.'

She riffled anxiously through the letters on her desk, and Lissa said, 'Don't worry about leaving things here. I'll stay and see to the phone.'

Rebecca seemed uncertain, and Lissa added, 'Really, it'll be all right. I shan't go off and leave the place unlocked.'

After a moment or two of hesitation, the other woman went over to the ledge and took down her bag. 'I don't suppose I shall be long,' she said, pocketing her keys. 'It isn't far to the hospital.'

After she had gone, Lissa went over to the security cupboard and took out a couple of files and two slim ledgers. Sliding them on to the desk, she snapped open her briefcase and took out her calculator.

Some time later, she acknowledged that the task was not proving to be as easy as she had expected. Pressing her fingers to the knot of tension at the back of her neck, she massaged gently, then stretched her limbs to relieve some of her aching muscles. For some reason, she was finding the last few pages difficult to sort out. Probably, she had been studying the figures with too much intensity, and now she needed a break.

The door opened, and as she watched Rourke breeze into the room she concluded wearily that fate must be conspiring against her. Why had he come back, out of the blue, to threaten her equilibrium even further?

'Where's Rebecca?' he asked curtly, coming over to deposit a large cardboard box on the table without regard for any of the documents scattered around. Quickly, Lissa gathered them up and dropped them in a heap on her opened briefcase. Obviously, he liked to work amidst clutter, and it wouldn't bother him if a few pages were creased. It was something she couldn't abide.

'She had to take some things over to the hospital for Adam.'

He grunted something unintelligible as he went to the security cupboard and slammed it shut, twisting his key in the lock.

'And why are you still here?' he demanded. 'There's no need for your presence if Rebecca isn't using the computer. You can work quite easily on anything else from your own office. Or were you hoping lover-boy might return?'

Lissa's control snapped. 'Just how many of your insulting remarks do you think I'm going to take?' she bit out angrily. 'Not only are you smearing my character with your vicious insinuations, but you're maligning a man who is your partner, a friend, not to mention your brother-in-law. Do you seriously expect that I could contemplate an assignation with a man whose wife is lying in a hospital bed?'

'Why not?' he grated, ramming his knuckles down on the desk. 'You don't appear to have any qualms about spending the weekend with him, or flaunting your relationship in front of her day by day. Why should the fact that she's ill and helpless make any difference? If you were going to worry about her feelings you wouldn't have started the affair in the first place.'

Her eyes glittered with rage. 'If I were a man,' she snapped furiously, 'you'd find yourself lucky to get away with a bloody nose. Don't judge me by your own standards. Just because you have no conscience about how you conduct your own affairs——'

'We are not discussing my affairs,' he cut in icily. 'I am not married, and I am not involved with anyone who is married. We're talking about the way my sister has been devastated by your constant and intimate contact with her husband.'

Lissa said with crushing force, 'Whether or not she is your sister gives you no right to make slanderous, evil accusations. My personal life is my own business, and if Adam wants his marriage to survive he should sort it out for himself. It has nothing whatever to do with you.'

'It has everything to do with me,' he said fiercely. 'The fact that you are here in my office gives me the right to ask questions and demand answers, and you're going to tell me what I want to know, Lissa.' His jaw clenched, his mouth made a taut, menacing line.

'Don't you try to threaten me,' she hit back. 'I'm sure you know very well why I'm here, unless you're living in another dimension. I'm working on a program for Adam. I should have thought he'd told you all about it by now, or don't you two ever communicate properly? He wants the business streamlining, to make it run more efficiently.'

'We don't need streamlining. We're doing fine as we are,' he growled. 'I don't want you here, sifting through the paperwork, upsetting the system, and generally getting in the way.'

'Adam thinks differently. He asked me to sort through the files and see if I could come up with something to make life easier.' She sniffed disparagingly. 'You may not have noticed, but he's running around trying to do the work of ten men.'

'That's because he hasn't learned to pace himself or to sort out what's important and what isn't. He doesn't need a new program, he needs a course on relaxation. And I don't mean with some titian-haired she-devil either.'

Her pencil rattled out a staccato rhythm on the desk-top, as she tossed it angrily to one side. 'Your rudeness is beyond belief,' she gritted. 'But then, I might have known you would take that attitude. In some areas you're as blinkered as a donkey. Let me make it clear. I'm here for one reason—to do a job, and I mean to carry it through to the best of my ability, with or without your approval. If you don't like it, take it up with Adam.'

'I might have expected you to hang on in there like a limpet,' Rourke said with a tight grimace. 'It suits your Scorpio mentality, doesn't it? Prying into what doesn't concern you, investigating in poky little corners.'

She stood up, facing him stiffly. 'And what makes you such an expert on the subject? Since when did you turn from an ignoramus into a know-all?'

His colour darkened, and he scowled, his jaw jutting aggressively. 'Being around you for any length of time, I'd sooner know what it is that makes you tick. That way, I can dodge the knives when they come.'

Her breath hissed through her teeth. 'Knife-throwing is not my forte. I don't belong in a circus.'

'No, and you don't belong here either. I want you out of this office, out of my hair. Is that quite clear, or do I have to spell it out?'

Her teeth bared in a tight smile. 'Why so adamant, I wonder? Are you afraid I'll interrupt your steamy sessions with your secretary? Pardon me for intruding. I'll go away and leave you to your fevered dalliances. That's what Pisceans are all about, isn't it?'

She turned away and his hand shot out to grip her wrist in a vice-like clamp. 'Let's leave Rebecca out of this, shall we? You've no call to go whingeing on about morals when you're making up to Adam in this very office. Thinking yourself in love is no excuse. You're out of line, lady, way out of line.'

'I am doing nothing of the sort. What do you know of love, who are you to decide what I feel? And let go of me.' She glowered at the fingers making a sharp imprint on her wrist.

'Like hell I will. What was that fiasco at the cottage all about, then? He didn't go to the trouble of setting up a little love-nest for nothing.' Rourke's blue eyes lanced through her like spears of ice. 'And what was going on in your mind? Was sleeping with him the price you had to pay for having him throw a little business your way?' He jerked her to him. 'You should have come to me, sweetheart, I'm the owner of the company. I'm the major shareholder. Who knows what you might have got if you'd played your hand right?'

His head came down and his mouth fastened on hers, cutting off the supply of air to her lungs, forcing her lips back against her teeth. The fingers of one hand curled around her neck, his thumb angled beneath her jaw to tip back her head. She tried to twist away from him, the buttons of her blouse giving way as she moved, but he was too strong; he imprisoned her within the steel band of his arm, dominating her body with the grinding pressure of his own. His lips savaged hers, his hand kneading the tender flesh at her hip as though he would make her one with him. A cry choked in her throat, and after an eternity he lifted his head, and stared down at her, his breath coming in harsh, roughened bursts.

Her mouth burned from the angry possession of that kiss, her lips were swollen, throbbing with tempestuous heat, and in the momentary stillness that followed they stood apart, facing each other like warriors poised in the midst of battle.

Her eyes had darkened to an intense, violent green, sparks flaring within their depths, and when he moved towards her once more she lifted her hand and hit him hard across the face, her palm cracking along his cheekbone with satisfying force. A bright red weal sprang up along the point of impact, a blaze of angry colour, and she watched it slowly spread, her breath rasping in her throat, her chest heaving raggedly.

'Don't try out your macho tactics on me,' she said hoarsely. 'I'd rather crawl on broken glass than have you manhandle me. Go find some other female to practise on.'

'Who did you have in mind? Rebecca?' His glittering gaze raked her slender form. 'That still rankles, doesn't it, Lissa? I wonder why? You might well rant and rage, and lash about with all the fury of a gathering storm, but underneath there are different vibes, making a commotion totally their own, aren't there? What exactly are you trying to hide? Maybe your immunity to me isn't as strong as you thought.'

He came a step closer and she gave a shaky laugh. 'Back to school, Einstein. I think you may have a fundamental flaw in your thought processes. Evidently you're mixing fact and fantasy again.'

'Am I? Or could it be that you are too frightened to own up to your own emotional weaknesses?' His hand went to the small of her back, pulling her to him once more in spite of her resistance. 'Let's find out, shall we?'

Her fingers jerked in trembling denial against his shirt front, and were softly crushed as his arms closed around her. She felt the light, warm caress of his breath on her cheek as he bent his head and murmured tauntingly, 'Just how much heat does it take to melt broken glass?'

Her mumbled protest was lost in the fierce burn of his mouth as it claimed hers. He ravished her senses, draining her of any will to fight, and then let his tongue flicker in lazy exploration along the full pink curve of her lips. 'You taste delicious,' he said huskily, 'like strawberries ripening in the sun.'

He kissed her again, testing the quivering softness of her response, until she yielded helplessly to the unhurried persuasion of his mouth, her lips clinging with aching, bitter-sweet desire. The kiss was different now, sensuous, infinitely pleasurable, leading her on a path of discovery towards a distant, hazy plateau, a focus for all the half-assuaged yearning that stirred within her.

His searching mouth made a languid foray to the silky disorder of her blouse, nudging aside the filmy material. She felt his smile whisper over the creamy swell of her breasts and then his lips began to feather along the lacy edge of her bra. Her breath caught and fragmented, a shuddery sigh that lingered in her throat.

'A sprinkling of golden sugar crystals,' he murmured. 'Does the rest of you taste as sweet, I wonder? I think I'd like to lick my way slowly over your luscious curves until I've sampled all the honeyed temptations you keep hidden away. Shall I do that, Lissa—shall I hunt out your secrets and make them my own?'

The glide of his hands was leisured and sure, and the wild sensations it evoked in her brought a hectic flush to her cheeks, startled a choked cry from her lips.

'Let me go,' she said hoarsely. 'I won't let you do this to me, Rourke; I won't let you use me this way.'

For a moment, she did not think he had heard. His lips hovered around the heavy swell of her breast, his palms sought out the rounded curve of her hips and angled her into his hard male thighs. 'I want to hear my name whispering over your lips,' he muttered thickly. 'I want to hear the soft sighs breaking from you when I make love to you. . .why should I stop now, when I know that you want it, too?'

'Because that's all it is. . .' she said, a catch in her voice. 'Wanting, moulding me to your desire, getting rid of a hunger that will be gone by nightfall.' She pushed at his chest to put some distance between them, pulling together the edges of her blouse with fingers that trembled. 'Afterwards, there would only be dislike and resentment, because you don't care for my feelings at all. You always think the worst of me. Every time I try to explain things you brush me aside as though nothing I say can have any validity.' She ran her hands shakily through her hair. 'I won't be used; I want more than that.'

His mouth twisted with cynicism, and he let her go, turning towards the desk. 'Words of love, you mean? Empty phrases to give you the illusion that it's Adam who's holding you, and not me? I don't think so, Lissa. I don't have the stomach for that. If you're suffering withdrawal symptoms, that's too bad, but don't expect me to help you.'

'I wouldn't expect anything from you. I said you

were blinkered, and it's true. You care deeply for your sister, but it's blinded you to everything else.' Her voice shattered, and she drew in a tremulous breath. 'You believe Emma is suffering, but it doesn't matter to you that I've worries of my own to contend with. You're not interested in my side of it. All you see is a challenge, a danger to your family that must be removed, in whatever way possible.'

Rourke's gaze was cool. 'Worries?' he queried. 'When did you ever tell me what was really going on in your head? Each time I asked, you fobbed me off, and now you're suggesting that I should fix my belief in you without some kind of hook to hang it on. It doesn't work that way. I know my sister, and I know Adam, and I'm clear in my mind that before you came along there were no outward signs that anything was amiss. If you want me to trust in you, you'll have to do more than protest your innocence, or you go it alone.'

She brought herself up stiffly, her shoulders lifting, her eyes shimmering with the brilliance of despair. 'Well, that's fine by me,' she said, moving around the desk like an automaton. 'I don't need you, I don't need anybody.' She rammed papers inside her brief-case, and snapped the lid shut. 'And now I've spent enough time here—I have clients to see.'

Making her way to the door, she flung it open, and walked out to the car park. As she went, she ransacked her bag for her keys, and almost bumped into Rebecca, coming in the opposite direction.

'Are you looking for these?' Rebecca asked, handing them over. 'I'm sorry, I took them by mistake.

They were next to mine, and in my hurry I picked up both sets.'

Lissa stared at her blankly for a moment. 'Thanks,' she muttered, before climbing into her car. She started up the engine and drove swiftly away. She did not look back.

CHAPTER SEVEN

IT WOULD have been better, Lissa thought unhappily, if she had avoided Lynx from the very beginning. Her involvement with Adam and Rourke had brought her nothing but trouble and recrimination so far, and when she looked ahead to the future she could see only a bleak landscape stretching out before her. It seemed that she could not be anywhere near Rourke without her emotions erupting all over the place. It left her weak and confused, totally disorientated, while he came away completely unscathed.

She would have to keep away from him, but how could she do that, when there was still this job for Adam to be finished?

Opening her briefcase, she stared down at the contents. What were these papers doing in here? In her haste to get away, she must have bundled up the documents and ledgers that she had been working on and brought them back with her. She sighed. It just went to show what a distraught state her mind had slipped into. She had even left her calculator behind. She gave another sigh. That would have to be retrieved, but tomorrow would be soon enough. In the meantime, she might just as well take another look at those ledgers and see if she could make any sense of them.

Adam phoned again the next day. 'Can you come

over?' he pleaded. 'I've a problem, and there's no one here to give me a hand. Rebecca's out, taking her daughter to the health centre, and I'd ask Rourke, but he's at the Brooksby plant again this morning.'

'Of course,' she promised. 'I need to collect my calculator anyway.' If Rourke was out, she could just about cope. He had used her cruelly, without compunction, to assuage his own needs. Hadn't he admitted it—that he had no time for love? All he had wanted was to slake his own desires, and she had been on hand, a willing and eager victim. Shame burnt a fiery path across her cheeks. It would happen no more, she determined. Rourke could not hurt her if she kept her distance.

Driving to the office, she strove to get herself under control once more. Would this be the opportunity to mention to Adam her difficulties over the ledgers? Something was wrong, but she hadn't quite been able to put her finger on it. Although she had made some photocopies to study later, it was possible that Adam might be able to clear the matter up in a few moments.

Parking the MG, she reached for her briefcase from the passenger seat, and then groaned inwardly. It wasn't there. She had left it sitting on the table in her flat, she remembered, thinking back. It was all Rourke's fault. If he didn't constantly barge in on her thoughts and drive everything else out of her head, she wouldn't be having any of these problems. She would just have to return the papers later in the week.

Adam was in a hurry, as usual. Explaining the

situation, he watched patiently enough while she dealt with the disk he needed, and then he said gratefully, 'Thanks, Lissa. I don't know what I'd do without you. I'm sorry I have to dash off again, but I'm due at Bartons in thirty minutes. I told them I'd get this disk to them. Don't rush off; stay and finish your coffee. I'll leave you a spare key for the office—then you could lock up for me when you leave.'

She gave him a wry smile, and sipped the hot liquid while he moved about the office like a whirlwind, gathering up various bits and pieces. When he had gone, she found her calculator and slipped it into her bag. Taking her cup and saucer over to the sink in the small kitchenette, she began to rinse them out under the tap. Perhaps she would get the chance later to talk to him about the ledgers.

Replacing the crockery in the cupboard, she walked back to the desk where she had left her bag, and stopped suddenly in her tracks, seeing Rourke's familiar figure looming ahead. Her heart gave a strange flip inside her ribcage, and she sucked in a deep breath to steady herself.

'I thought you were out this morning,' she said diffidently, her eyes taking in the slanting twist of his mouth.

'But now I'm back,' he murmured, his voice cool, 'and just in time, I see.'

Her chin lifted. 'I was just about to go,' she told him, keeping a firm grip on herself. At all costs, she had to keep calm.

'So soon?' His blue glance shifted over her.

'I only came to collect my calculator.' She would

not mention Adam. We're like strangers, she thought, remote, cool, two people who greet each other with surface politeness; but inside she felt numb, as though nothing could touch her any more. She started to walk towards the door, and his deep, gravel-timbered voice held her back.

'I think you should stay a while. We need to talk.'

Over her shoulder she said, 'Somehow, I don't think that would be a good idea.'

'You wouldn't,' he said tersely. 'But I think you should, all the same.' He came to her and placed a hand beneath her elbow. 'Come through the workshop to my office.'

'No.' Lissa shook her head. 'I really do have to leave now.'

His mouth made a hard straight line. 'But I insist. Whatever you have in mind can wait a while.'

'A typically arrogant assumption.' She tried to tug her arm away, but he ignored her struggles, leading her into a small, plush-carpeted room furnished simply with a desk and bookcase, a couple of armchairs, and a long, padded couch set back along one wall.

'There's nothing we have to say to each other,' she protested with irritation, 'and I'm not in the mood for any more of your accusations. Besides, I have work to do.'

'Stop arguing with me, and sit down.'

Stubbornly, she resisted, and Rourke's breath hissed impatiently through his teeth. Taking hold of her shoulders, he pushed her down on to the couch. 'Do as you're told, for once in your life. And don't stiffen up, for heaven's sake; anyone would think I was about to leap on you.'

She raised a fine, dark brow, and his mouth tightened. 'You're quite safe,' he muttered. 'I haven't savaged anyone in weeks.'

'That could be a matter for debate,' she said with curt emphasis, watching him prowl up and down like a shark testing the boundaries of a tank. Any moment the glass would come crashing down.

His eyes glittered fiercely. 'What's that supposed to mean? Just because I may have been a little short-tempered of late——'

She gave a small, harsh laugh and he glowered at her. 'Is it any wonder if I am?' he demanded. 'A saint would be forgiven for losing his cool around you.' A snarl framed his mouth. 'Adam never stood a chance, did he, once you came back on the scene? It was bad enough that he had this damn-fool obsession with programming—if he had got his priorities right in the first place, he and Emma might have made some headway.' He began to move again, his feet making tracks in the blue wool carpet. 'As it is, this new crisis they're having to face might be the thing to push them towards solving their difficulties. Just make sure you keep away from him. Emma will be coming home soon, and I don't want her upset—I don't want you on the scene. Is that understood?'

Lissa's features were carved in ice. 'Perfectly. You've made yourself crystal-clear.' She stood up. 'And now, if you've quite finished, I'll go.'

He pushed her down into the chair. 'Sit,' he commanded.

'I am not a dog,' she said sharply, baring her teeth, 'but I may well bite. You might be wise to think on that.'

He studied her coldly. 'I'll remember to keep my distance. In the meantime, there are things I have to say to you.'

Her brow rose in a finely sculpted arch. 'Are there, indeed? I fail to see why I should stay and subject myself to any more of your murderous mood.' Obviously his relationship with Rebecca was undergoing problems and his temper was suffering as a result. No doubt the other woman had been regarding her with covert suspicion all along—and who could wonder at her resentment when her lover was such a fickle character? 'Why don't you try taking out your frustrations on a squash court?' she suggested with acid vigour. 'It might prove to be a far more satisfying exercise than baiting me.'

'My frustrations,' he said tautly, 'would be alleviated by a little co-operation from you. You have the uncanny knack of getting under my skin and raising my temperature to an uncomfortable degree.' His teeth set. 'Why are you so keen to work on this program? From what Adam tells me, you have plenty of other clients. You don't need this work above all else.'

'That's hardly a businesslike approach, is it? If I pick and choose at this stage, I'm not likely to get off the ground. Why are you so set against the idea? It doesn't interfere with your side of things, does it? From what I gather, you're more interested in development projects—though I don't know why you bother, since you'll never be satisfied with anything you come up with—if you had your wits about you, you'd be marketing your ideas, not sitting on them.'

His lips thinned. 'I told you, they're not ready yet. When I'm happy with them, I'll do what's necessary.'

She gave a disbelieving sniff. 'Pigs might fly. And I fail to see why someone with such an inventive, lively mind as yours can be so dog-in-the-manger about updating things in the office. It doesn't make sense. Rebecca's life could be made ten times easier with the programs I can work out for her.'

'That's just the point,' he said flatly. 'For someone like you, who knows computers inside out and backwards, there's no problem. But Rebecca doesn't have that aptitude; she gets herself in a state about any new technology. Apart from which, she has enough on her plate at the moment. Living alone and trying to bring up a small daughter is no easy task, and taking extra time to learn a new skill is just an added burden.'

Lissa was silent for a moment, thinking, then she said, 'She seems to me to be a normally intelligent woman. Have you thought about getting a temp in to do her job, while she goes on a course? With the proper training behind her, she would feel much more confident.'

'Hmm.' Rourke turned the idea over in his mind. 'You may well be right. I'll give it some thought.'

He would, Lissa reflected numbly. His concern for Rebecca was something tangible, and it left a heavy dragging weight in her own heart. An ache that she dared not examine too closely.

'Why is it,' he enquired, 'that we always finish up arguing? It seems to me that things have a nasty habit of going haywire around you.' He came and sat down beside her on the couch. 'Maybe it's time I learned a little more about you, about what makes you tick. Those worries you mentioned the other day, for instance—the ones you keep pushing to one side.'

She began to pluck imaginary fibres from her skirt. 'I don't know why I said that,' she muttered. 'Anyway, if you harbour such great objections to my being in your office, why on earth should you take the slightest interest in my problems? The two things simply don't add up.'

He studied her thoughtfully. 'It isn't your presence in my office that disturbs me. Merely the fact that Adam happens to be there, too. Now, can we cut out the delaying tactics and get on with it? I'd like to know what these problems are.'

Lissa blinked, momentarily distracted. 'Nothing of any importance. Only the usual day-to-day things that get to everyone after a while. Probably the trials and tribulations of running a business.'

'No. That won't do, Lissa,' he said, his tone brisk. 'You're being evasive again, and I won't have it. I'm not going to let you fob me off. Come on, out with it. This has gone on long enough.'

'I always said you had a vivid imagination,' she side-stepped. 'Everything's fine, everything's coming up roses.'

He shook his head. 'Not so. Those roses smell very iffy to me, and I want to know what's going on.' He fixed her with a cool stare. 'I mean to find out, even if it entails keeping you here indefinitely, so you might as well start talking and get it over with. And you can forget the black looks; I mean business.'

Moodily, she pursed her lips. 'I don't know what's going on,' she said in exasperation. 'If I did, there wouldn't be a problem.' She lapsed into an aggrieved silence.

Rourke sat back, stretching out his long legs. 'Go on,' he said. 'Get on with it.' he interlocked his fingers behind his head, his attitude one of complete relaxation.

'I'd hate to keep you awake,' she muttered sourly.

His mouth quirked. 'I think better this way,' he murmured. 'Spill the beans. What's on you mind?'

Reluctantly she gave in to his badgering. 'Someone doesn't want me here, in Eastlake,' she said, her voice low. 'I don't know why, and I don't know who—and it was probably nothing anyway; I probably magnified it in my head out of all proportion.'

'What happened?'

She told him about the notes, the broken glass and spilled wine that had shaken her so much at the time. 'It's as though someone hates me,' she said, 'and I don't know what I've done to make anyone feel that way.'

He looked at her thoughtfully. 'The wine glass was in the conservatory, you said? I suppose any number of people could have seen you leave it there.'

Lissa gave a little shiver. 'It makes me cold just to think of someone watching me, following me. I suppose if I hadn't gone back into that room they'd have found some other way of leaving the message.' She rubbed at her arms, chafing the cotton sleeves of her blouse. 'As it is, I've no way of knowing who is behind it all, so there isn't much point fretting over it, is there? I'd be far better employed in getting on with some work.' She made a move to get to her feet and Rourke's hand stopped her.

'Not so fast. Calm down and stay where you are. All right, so it's a mystery, and there's not a lot you can do to get to the heart of it yet, but you don't have to let it get to you. Just sit back and take it easy while I think.'

She subsided into silence for a few minutes, her glance going around the room, her fingers twining restlessly in her lap until his hand reached out and covered hers.

'Stop it,' he said.

'Have you thought of something?'

'I'm working on it. In the meantime——' He slid an arm around her waist, pulling her into the warm circle of his embrace. 'Perhaps this will take your mind off it.'

His kiss took her by surprise, caught her off-balance. The warmth and gentleness coaxed her surrender, subduing her inner turmoil and replacing it with something that was infinitely more disturbing. The smooth glide of his fingers down her spine was enticing and her treacherous body curved sensuously against him. Her breasts grazed his chest, the small tight nubs hardening with the delicate, tantalising friction.

Her mouth softened and trembled beneath his. His

hands stroked and tantalised, sought out the hidden, sensitive places, and aroused in her longings that she had never before experienced. How could he make her feel this way? It was like being adrift on a warm sea, floating on a slow, swelling tide that would eventually wash up on a sun-kissed beach in little breakers of sparkling foam. She felt the silken warmth eddy around her, seducing her deep into its unfathomed depths. Where was he taking her? Did he feel it too, this bathing of their twin souls in their own primeval element? She almost wanted to cry, he made her so intensely aware, showed her what ecstasies there might be in store. . .

His breath whispered softly against her cheek, his lips trailing along the smooth column of her throat. 'I want to look at you, Lissa,' he muttered huskily. His fingers stole to the buttons of her blouse, loosening their fragile hold on the flimsy cotton. 'I've waited so long, I've dreamed about you, about your loveliness.' The front fastening of her bra fell apart beneath his light touch and her breasts spilled out, full and round, aching for the brush of his lips across their creamy slopes.

'Beautiful,' he murmured, 'beautiful little rosebuds, just waiting for my kiss. Shall I kiss you, Lissa, shall I pay homage to those ripe, exotic fruits you've kept hidden from me for so long? How shall I touch you? Like this? Tell me what I should do, what will pleasure you.'

She gasped as his lips closed over the taut mound of her breast, her body sensitised, waiting, begging for his caress. The flick of his tongue teased and tormented her, lapped at the edges of her self-control. Her body throbbed, her nerve-endings tingled with little darts of fire.

'Rourke,' she whispered, 'I want. . . I don't know . . .help me, I——' She broke off as his mouth tugged gently, suckled, moved over her breasts to nudge and explore, spreading flame and desire like a raging thirst that must be quenched.

'I've wanted you,' he said, his voice rasping against her skin, 'since the first moment I saw you. You were standing by the boat, demanding that I let you on board, and I felt such a raw, aching need lance through me that it shocked me. Then you started on with that high-handed act, and I felt a tremendous urge to tame your proud spirit, hear your soft whimpering sighs as I buried myself in you. You can't know how much I've wanted you, Lissa.'

She lowered her head, hiding her flushed cheeks with the tawny curtain of her hair. No, she had not known how much he had held himself in check, but what lay behind his pursuit of her? Was it only a desire for conquest? What did he really feel for her? Could it be anything more than a compulsion to take the eternal conflict between the sexes to the ultimate battleground? He wanted to gain her total submission, a mastery of her that was complete and overwhelmingly final, and she knew, instinctively, that such an achievement was not beyond his power. He could command her responses as easily as though he held her in thrall, and that made her more than a little afraid.

'Rourke, what. . .?' She lifted her gaze to him once

more, but he hushed her with a finger pressed lightly to her lips.

'I heard something, someone,' he muttered. 'Didn't you hear it, too? The outer door?'

She shook her head wordlessly. She had been deaf and blind to everything except what had passed between them. Yet he had remained alert the whole time, his senses tuned, even in their intimacy; he had been able to bring his mind to other things.

A sickness clawed inside her. How had she let herself be so deluded? When would she ever learn that vital lesson? She had allowed him to entice her into what was, to him, nothing more than a seduction scene, where she had been primed and ripe for the taking. The knowledge was the taste of ashes in her mouth.

He said tautly, 'It must be Rebecca. You'd better tidy yourself up. I'll go and talk to her.'

He was cool and terse, and it was clear to Lissa what was going on in his mind. He did not want his girlfriend to know how he had deceived her with another woman. His traits were written in the stars, and he could not deny them, but he did not want to suffer the inconvenience of being found out.

She watched him leave the room, her heart heavy, as though she had run a long way uphill, and had not the strength for the return journey. Sooner or later Rebecca would learn that her trust in him was unfounded, that she had to share him with any woman who took his fancy. He did not believe in love. Hadn't he said that to express it would be just empty words? Love was too complicated an emotion for him; it required too much staying power.

Fighting back the sting of bitter tears, Lissa straightened her clothes, and left the office by a back door. She did not want to face either of them—the pain of her own betrayal went too deep for that, and she wanted only to be left alone, to deal with her heartache as best she could.

There were times, Lissa reflected, when she might have preferred a more mundane job, where her thoughts could wander unhindered along different by-ways. But she did not have that luxury. Running her own business meant that there was no let-up, no time for sliding into a slough of self-pity and morbid reconstruction of events that sapped her energy.

Rourke had made no move to contact her after she had left the office yesterday morning, and that had to mean that she had been right in her assumptions. He did not want to see her again, and be faced with his own guilt.

She attacked the computer keyboard with renewed vigour. It was her folly to be attracted to the wrong kind of man, but perhaps one day she might learn her lesson. First Richard Blake had taken advantage of her innocence, seducing her into a youthful infatuation from which she had managed to free herself only just in time. And now Rourke. What Richard had done was nothing compared to the havoc that Rourke had created within her. He was playing with her emotions, stringing them out like a taut band that would snap at the slightest pressure. She hated him for what he was doing to her. He had worked out her vulnerability and was intent on exploiting it to the full. He was heartless, an unfeeling, treacherous monster, and she hated him.

The computer bleeped at her indignantly, and she gave it a mutinous scowl. So she was pressing the wrong keys; did it have to make such a racket? Was everything conspiring against her? Was it her fault if her brain wouldn't function at a normal level? Rourke was to blame for all the horrors she had to contend with. Ever since she had met him she had been on a roller-coaster, going up and down and swerving from one emotional crisis to another. How could she be expected to cope with stupid computers that hadn't the wit to understand a simple error, or calculators that came up with the wrong numbers? They could all go hang; she'd switch them off and go and submerge herself in the bath for half an hour.

Pinning up her wayward curls, Lissa made a face in the steam-coated bathroom mirror. A soak in a hot tub, brimming with scented foam, was about the only thing that could soothe her wounded spirits. She dropped her robe on to the stool near by and stepped into the water, sinking slowly down into the warmth. Why did life have to be so complicated? It wasn't fair to have to cope with all this turmoil.

Angling the toes of one leg towards the ceiling, she absently studied its soap-sleeked length. What did he see in Rebecca anyway? A blonde, blue-eyed doll for him to play with; that was about the size of it. She threw the sponge at the taps in disgust, and registered the peal of the doorbell at the same time.

She might have guessed that as soon as she tried for a little peace and quiet the whole place would be inundated with callers. From the repeated ringing, it was probably someone she owed money to. Surely she'd paid the rent a couple of weeks back?

With a frustrated sigh, she towelled herself dry and pulled on her robe over her underwear. People were a pain. She'd have done better to drown her sorrows in a bottle of red wine, and let the world go to blazes. Her mouth made a wry twist.

Rourke's thumb was still pressed to the bell as she opened the door, and they stared at each other, he, frowning, she with an expression of wary mistrust.

'What do you want?' she asked flatly.

'To iron a few things out.' He strode past her into the hall and flicked a glance around. 'Where's the sitting-room—through here?' He marched to the lounge and stood by the large bay window, glaring at her furnishings.

'If my décor offends your sensibilities, you could always leave,' she said curtly.

'Don't try to be facetious; it doesn't suit you.' His eyes narrowed on her. 'What were you doing at Lynx yesterday, before I came along?'

His question startled her. 'I left my calculator, I told you; I went to pick it up.'

'And what else did you collect while you were there?'

'I don't understand.' She stared at him, her green eyes puzzled. 'What are you getting at?'

'I want to know what you brought away with you,

apart from your calculator,' he rasped. 'That's clear enough, isn't it?'

'Nothing; I've already said—I stopped by because Adam asked me to copy a disk for him, and then I looked for my calculator—I left it on the table the other day.'

'So Rebecca's lying when she says you have the financial ledgers and a couple of files out of the security cupboard, is she?' He ground the words out as though he were chewing on granite.

'Ledgers? Oh. . .' She had forgotten all about them; how could she have let something so important slip her mind? 'I meant to——'

'You meant to do what? Are you saying now that you do have them? What's the matter with you? Is your memory completely addled, or am I caught up in the middle of a prize piece of double-dealing?'

'Double-dealing? Are you quite mad, as well as totally lacking in any of the trappings of civilised society? Don't think you can barge in here harassing me like this,' she snapped, 'shooting questions at me as if you were taking part in a firing squad.' If he hadn't rattled her so much the other day, leaving her high and dry to sneak off and join his girlfriend, she might have remembered to tell him about the dratted ledgers. He had absolutely no business forcing his way in here and treating her like a criminal.

'Do you have them?' His mouth was tight, his jaw set in anger.

'Yes,' she seethed, 'I have them. I was going to return them to you.'

'And in the meantime you've finished working on a project for your good friend Richard Blake?'

Her brow lifted. 'Is that any of your concern?'

'Quite possibly. Some might wonder,' he grated, 'whether Blake will now be able to set his prices at a level low enough to undermine Lynx. Only time will tell, won't it?'

She stared at him in shock. 'You're accusing me of—of spying, of industrial espionage?' She took in a deep, shuddery breath. Was there no end to the horrors he thought her capable of? Bitterness shafted through her like a knife, her eyes darkening with angry frustration. 'How dare you come here throwing around such dirty lies? Don't you have any faith in me at all? Do you seriously believe that I would jeopardise my career by dabbling in such nasty, underhand acts?' Fury gathered in her head like a cloaking red mist. 'Let me tell you, Deveraugh,' She gritted, her voice shaking with anger, 'I've had just about all I can stomach of your malicious slanders. I've done nothing to deserve all your vicious insinuations—neither with Richard, nor with Adam, and if you can't bring yourself to believe in me the least you could do would be to grant them some scrap of integrity.'

Storming over to the table, she snatched up her briefcase and flicked it open. 'These are what you came for, aren't they—your ledgers, a couple of files? I don't believe I have anything else, except for a few photocopies. But don't take my word for it; perhaps you should search the place, just in case. Maybe I have a filing cabinet stuffed under the mat. Why don't you check? Or perhaps I shoved the contents of your safe inside my robe when I saw you at the door. You've just no way of knowing how low I'll stoop, have you?'

A growl broke in his throat, and he started towards her.

'Get away from me,' she raged. 'I don't want you near me; I want you out of this flat and out of my life, do you hear? And you can take these with you——' She flung the contents of the case at him, and watched with satisfaction as she made a direct hit. 'I don't want anything to do with you, or anything remotely connected with you,' she railed. 'I wouldn't soil my hands. Take your rotten papers— and go to hell. You can burn in the fires of the damned for all I care. Get out of here!'

CHAPTER EIGHT

I OUGHT to have taken heed of the warnings contained in those anonymous horoscopes, Lissa thought morosely, fingering the disks she had prepared for Adam. Hadn't everything gone wrong from the moment she had come back to Eastlake? Perhaps she ought to go away, and make a new start somewhere else. If she stayed here, there would always be the torment of running into Rourke, and stirring up all the pain and unhappiness that loving him had brought. For she did love him. Though her temper had run away with her, and she had sent him away, she could not deny that the grim coldness of his departure had left a barren place in her heart.

He hated her; that was why he had made those foul accusations when surely he must know she was not capable of such treachery. There was only so much she could take, and she did not know just when her breaking-point might come.

It was not so easy, though, to uproot herself, just as she was beginning to get established here. There were so many loose ends, so many clients still waiting for attention, and she could not let them down. All she could do was to give Adam the completed programs, and then keep as far away as possible from Lynx and the man who ran it.

There was, too, the problem of the discrepancies

she had found in those ledgers. In all fairness, she should point out the entries that were suspect, so that they could find out what was amiss. That one final journey she would make to clear up all her obligations to Adam and Rourke, and that would be an end. She would cut the cord that bound her to them cleanly and irrevocably.

When she arrived at Lynx some hours later she found that the door to the office was propped open, and as soon as she entered she understood the reason. The acrid smell of smoke clung about the place, black smudges streaking the walls and the floor where a fire had burned itself out. Charcoal remnants of paper littered the floor and desk-tops, and she saw that the steel drawer of the cabinet was hanging open.

'If you're here to see Adam,' Rourke said, as Lissa walked dazedly across the soot-blackened carpet, 'you're in for a disappointment. He's bringing Emma home from hospital this afternoon. We don't expect him back here until tomorrow.'

'What happened?' Lissa asked, looking around the room in disbelief. The polished surface of the dark mahogany desk was charred and pitted beyond all redemption, the wood splintered and rough. 'Does he know about this?'

'He knows.' The words were clipped and terse, and she turned, wide-eyed, to face him. 'He'll stay away because I've ordered him to stay away. Emma is his main concern right now. This is something we can deal with well enough without him.' His glance raked her sharply. 'Why have you come? Did you decide that you went too far? You desperately needed to see me, maybe even to take back some of the things you said?'

She winced inwardly at his abrasive tone. He had no feelings for her. His jeering remarks had hidden barbs, and just went to prove how little he cared either way. Coolly, she said, 'I wanted to talk to Adam about something. I've brought him the programs he asked for.'

'Give them to me. I'll deal with them.' He held out his hand, and she hesitated a moment, before searching in her bag for the disks. He wanted to be rid of her, to have her out of the office and out of his life, and that was what she wanted too, wasn't it? There was no trust between them, no meeting of minds.

She handed over the small package, and then ran her gaze once more over the chaos in the office. 'What happened here?'

'What does it look like?' he snapped. 'We had a visitation, a welcoming note from a pyromaniac.'

She stared at him in silence, chilled by the frozen wastes reflected in his eyes, and he said raspingly, 'The fires of the damned, wasn't that how you put it? Is this what you wanted? Does this satisfy your thirst for revenge?'

Lissa swallowed hard, remembering her words. Surely he did not blame her for this? 'How can you think it?' she said. 'Don't you know me at all?'

His laugh was harsh as he stepped towards her. 'Oh, yes, I know you very well, my beautiful tormentor. You'd like to see me suffer, wouldn't you?' He reached for her and his hands cruelly threaded her hair, slowly winding the bright strands around his fingers. Uncertain of his mood, she tried to pull away, but his hold on her tightened. 'Do you think I don't know what you're about? You stoke the flames with all the tantalising lures of Eve, and then you stand back and laugh while I burn in your heat. Isn't that the truth? Isn't that how you get your kicks?'

The blood stormed inside her head, pounding against her temples. 'I never did that,' she muttered hoarsely. 'You make me sound like some kind of tease—it was never that way——'

'Wasn't it? Maybe you do it without even trying.' He dragged her towards him, their bodies meeting in a violent collision that startled the breath from her. Shock, electric and swift, charged through her. He stared down at her upturned face, her soft pink lips parted on a gasp.

'You're hurting me,' she said, renewing her wild struggles to break free from his steely grip.

'I want to hurt you,' he rasped, his voice thick. 'I want to crush you, to take everything you have.' His mouth met hers with bruising force, and the clamour inside her head rose to a deafening crescendo, the world twisted and turned, tossing her adrift with the turbulence of a whirlwind. Then, abruptly, he released her and she fell back, her breathing fierce, her pulse thundering out of control.

'Why?' she demanded angrily. 'Why did you do that? Do you think you can vent your temper on me just as you please? I won't have it, do you hear? If Rebecca isn't inclined to ease your fevered libido then that's too bad. You'll have to make do with a cold shower or a dip in the lake, because I'm not available, do you understand? Are you getting my message?'

'It's getting through all right,' Rourke bit out harshly. 'Loud and clear. And so are the other signals—the ones you think I can't read. I know you, Lissa; I know you far better than you think, and I know exactly what's going on in that secretive labyrinth of a mind. You don't fool me for a second.'

'Is that so?' she slammed back, seething at his brash presumption. 'And I suppose that with your superior knowledge you've worked out that this—scene of devastation——' she flung a careless hand in the general direction of the office '—is all down to me. The possibility of it being accidental doesn't even arise, does it? Not for you the simple explanation of a dropped cigarette end or some such——'

'It would have to have been a very strange accident,' he cut in grimly, 'to have singled out the contents of the security cupboard for its main target, wouldn't you agree?'

'I thought you kept it locked?'

His expression was wintry. 'Obviously someone squeezed in through the keyhole and dropped a match among the paperwork.'

'I don't see any call for sarcasm,' Lissa said stiffly.

'You wouldn't,' he returned with brittle emphasis. 'It isn't your files that have gone up in smoke. Lord knows, it took long enough to compile all the information stored in there. This is the last thing we needed.'

A choked sound came from the doorway. Rebecca stood there, crying quietly, slow tears winding their way down her cheeks. 'It wasn't my fault,' she sniffed. 'The lock wasn't very good—you know it wasn't. The man was coming to look at it, only now. . .' She hiccuped, and sniffed again, little sobs choking in her throat.

Rourke went over to her and drew her towards a chair. Once she was seated, he put his arms around her, cradling her fair head against his chest. The girl whimpered into his shirt, and Lissa began to feel sick. He was always finding some excuse to hold that wretched girl. Why was it that his sympathy and understanding always went out to other women? All she ever had from him was the biting lash of his tongue.

'It's all right, Rebecca,' he muttered. 'No one's blaming you. There was nothing of real value destroyed. It was just a nuisance, that's all. Dry your tears.'

She hiccuped again, and Rourke looked around the office distractedly, a grimace shaping his mouth. 'Where's the damn coffee percolator disappeared to? You'd have thought our visitor would have left that intact. Breaking and entering's one thing, making off with essentials is another matter altogether.'

Rebecca dabbed at her eyes with a handkerchief. 'It wasn't a break-in, though, was it? You said this morning you couldn't see where anyone had forced their way in.'

'Did I?' He scowled, and pushed his hands in his pockets, beginning to pace the room. 'I said a lot of things this morning. Among them, where's the telephone book, where's the lead to the computer, and where's the spare kettle? None of which has been answered yet, I might add. Especially the last one, and you should know by now that I don't function well without caffeine.' He sent a glower in Lissa's direction.

'Don't look at me,' she said, still smarting from the display of affection he made towards his damp-eyed secretary. 'If I had any coffee, I'd probably pour it all over you.'

Rebecca frowned. She said to Rourke, 'You wanted to know if I'd lent out keys to anyone—the telephone engineer, you said, and the man who came to see to the new extension around the back.' She paused, her blue eyes slanting in Lissa's direction. 'Miss Holbrook had a key. In fact, I don't believe that she's handed it back yet.'

Lissa blinked, stunned by the veiled accusation. She looked at Rourke, and saw that his eyes had narrowed on her, glimmering faintly. He had no right to look at her that way. She had done nothing wrong, yet between them Rourke and Rebecca were making her feel like public enemy number one.

Into the silence she said, 'Yes, that's true, I do have a key. Adam gave it to me the other day so that I could lock up. I also have a key to the security cupboard.' Tearing open a pocket in her bag, she took out the offending objects and thrust them towards Rourke. 'Does that make me a suspect?' she asked, her spine rigid.

He did not answer, but then, there was no need for words. The granite control he exerted over his features said it all as he clipped the keys to his own ring.

'I can see that it does,' she said tightly, against the painful constriction of her throat. 'What motive would I have had?' How could he believe that she would have done such a thing? 'It's true that I had the opportunity to be alone in the office, and we both know that I was angry and said a lot of things in the heat of the moment. . .but would I really be this vindictive?'

Rourke's blue eyes assessed her coolly. 'The sting in the tail of the scorpion? Yes, you did have a lot to say for yourself, didn't you? Consigning me to hell seemed to make up the bulk of it, as I recall. Do I take it that I'm to be redeemed from that particular fate? I dare say, though, knowing you as I do, that it's only because you've thought up some other diabolical venegeance to inflict on me.'

'And destroying your files was just the beginning?' Her mouth moved in a tiny spasm of denial and unhappiness. There was no way she could prove her innocence, and he was certainly not open to giving her any benefit of the doubt. The whole thing was like a nightmare, growing out of all proportion. There had to be some way to break out of it and get back to reality.

She said carefully, 'There is, of course, another way of looking at it, if you can bear, for a moment, to push to one side the thought that there might have been any spiteful intent on my part.'

He lifted a dark brow. 'Such as?'

Lissa breathed in deeply. She had not intended to

bring this out into the open in quite this way, but she was left with little option, and she had a vague instinct that in the long run it might reap results. 'Who knows,' she murmured, 'what a thorough scrutiny of your books might have revealed? Perhaps there was something not quite right about the files and the ledgers. Maybe your accounts weren't as accurate as they should have been.' Her green eyes flickered. 'Are you by any chance due for a visit from the tax man or the VAT inspector in the near future?'

He frowned darkly. 'You're saying the fire was started in order to get rid of any incriminating evidence? There's an awful lot of supposition there, don't you think?' His tone was sceptical, as she might have expected. He was determined to dismiss anything that she had to say.

Rebecca pushed her handkerchief into her pocket. 'Anyone could come up with a story like that once the proof has been destroyed. Especially when the finger is being pointed at them.' She smoothed down the skirt of her linen suit, slowly crossing one long slender leg over the other. Rourke's head turned, his gaze following the action.

Lissa's nails bit convulsively into her palms. How could he do this to her? How could he allow himself to be diverted, when her integrity was at stake? Rebecca was accusing her of starting the fire, and he was doing nothing to dispute the idea. Was he so besotted with the woman that he couldn't see the fallibility of what she was saying?

She said huskily, 'Surely you can't really think that I had anything to do with this?'

He dragged his gaze away, and shrugged, leaning on a corner of the table, half sitting there. 'I'm sure the police will sort it all out eventually. No doubt they will want to interview you at some time. They've already taken fingerprints and all the other bits and pieces they thought necessary.'

Lissa's lashes swept downwards, hiding the hurt that filled her eyes. He was quite prepared to find her guilty, and he did not care. He was so cool now, so calm, and the fact that she was feeling utterly wretched did not bother him a bit. It would probably please him if she went to prison, because then she would be out of his hair, and he would be free to amuse himself to his heart's content with his pretty, blue-eyed doll.

Rebecca said, 'I'm sure the police will be interested to hear your tale. Though it's not very likely they'll take much notice, since you have no facts to go along with it.'

Lissa's chin lifted, her jaw firming as she viewed the other woman with dislike. She did not need to have that pointed out to her. She was neither blind, nor stupid. Any fool could see that with the ledgers and papers destroyed there was nothing to substantiate any misdealings with the accounts. But that wasn't the case, was it. . . ?

She said slowly, 'Actually, that isn't quite true. There is, in fact, a way that I can prove something was wrong.' Her glance went to Rourke. 'Those papers I gave you the other evening——'

'Gave?' he queried, his mouth edged with scorn.

'Wouldn't threw at me be a more apt way of phrasing it?'

Impatiently, she said, 'When you went off with those papers, there was something you left behind. If you hadn't been in such a foul temper——'

'Me?' he echoed, his tone scathing. 'In a temper? I suppose you were all sweetness and light, weren't you?'

'If you hadn't been so nasty,' she went on, ignoring his cold rebuttal, 'I'd probably have gathered everything up. As it is, Rebecca's quite right: if I'm to prove my innocence in all this, I'm sure the police will want something more to go on than just my conjecture.' Briefly, she glanced at the other woman, then looked down at her watch. 'It's rather late in the day now, though, to go bothering them with it. They probably change shifts round about this time. But tomorrow, first thing, I'll see to it that they are in full possession of the facts.'

Rebecca's blue gaze rested on her thoughtfully. 'Well, at least that solves that little problem,' she said. 'Though it does pose another one. . . What could possibly have been wrong with the books? Nothing of any importance, I'm sure, or Adam and Rourke would have noticed. Unless of course, you're accusing them of rigging things?'

Her brow lifted, and when Lissa made no reply she smiled dismissively, and stood up, her body long and graceful, the linen suit emphasising her willowy perfection. Rourke's head shifted once more, and he watched her as she moved towards the cabinet, admiring the model-girl walk, the slow, easy sway of her hips.

She pushed the drawer shut, and then turned back to look at him, her spine arching lightly against the cabinet, a subtle invitation in the pose. 'We really ought to make a start on getting this place cleaned up, you know. Then, perhaps, we can get back to normal.'

Rourke gave her an answering smile, his mouth curving attractively, but Lissa did not hear his murmured reply. She swung round and walked swiftly out of the office. Let them play their flirtatious games. She did not have to stay and watch.

Evening had begun to cast long grey shadows around the red-bricked building when Lissa arrived back at her flat. She had driven for miles, trying to throw off the demons of jealousy and bitter resentment that plagued her, but it was no use. Wherever she went, there would always be the knowledge deep within her that she loved Rourke, and that he did not love her in return. Nothing would shake that. It would remain with her forever, locked in the innermost corners of her being, a dull, aching pain that could never be assuaged.

She walked into the flat, and shrugged wearily out of her jacket, hanging it up in the closet. The gas burned with a flickering blue light as she switched on the fire in the sitting-room, and for a while she held out her hands to the flame. She was very cold. Inside, she was frozen, her body numb, her mind bleak, like an Arctic winter.

Going through to the kitchen, she made herself a

hot drink, and carried it into the room where the fire was at last beginning to heat up the air a little. She had not eaten that day, she recalled, but still she was not hungry. The thought of food made her feel nauseous.

She wondered how long it would be before Rebecca paid her nocturnal visit to the flat. For she would come; Lissa was almost certain of it.

Rebecca, for some reason, had altered the pages in those books. And she did not want anyone to find out what she had done.

Lissa had brought things out into the open, but it was too late now for regrets. Rebecca believed that Lissa could bring about her downfall, and she was almost bound to try to do something about it.

Why could Rourke not see the truth for himself? Was he so wrapped up in his beautiful secretary that it blinded him to everything?

Hollow-eyed, she stared into the fire. Rebecca had him panting after her. The woman was taking him for a ride, working on him to get what she wanted, and that included Lissa's destruction.

Her situation was perilous; she realised that. There was no way of knowing just how far the tight band of Rebecca's control would stretch, or to what extremes she would be driven. The night forces were at work here, dark and menacing, and Lissa was the bait, caught in a trap of her own making.

Why could Rourke not see how much she needed him? Her heart ached to have him with her right now, but that was a futile hope, born of despair. He had pulled her down with him into the whirlpool of love, and now that she was submerged and drowning he had left her, escaping through the cloaking mist that hung over the water. Rebecca lured him to her side, and he went willingly, his mind fogged by the cloudy veil that Neptune had thrown over him.

He did not hear Lissa calling to him across the haze that separated them, and he would not come to her. She was alone now, and he was lost to her forever.

CHAPTER NINE

THE flat was shrouded in darkness. A hushed, sleeping stillness had long since settled like a heavy blanket over the place, but Lissa stirred quietly in the depths of the armchair. It had been the faintest of sounds, but it was enough to bring her slowly to her feet, alert and expectant. Her ear was tuned to every creak and rustle that disturbed the air, and when it came again, that soft, almost imperceptible shuffling, she caught it, and her pulse-beat quickened. Silently, her fingers searched in the dim light, feeling her way, moving over the polished surface of the table, then, straightening, she went and stood by the side of the door, a slender, pale figure, waiting in the shadows of the night.

The door opened, and her presentiments were realised as someone moved stealthily across the carpeted floor, the narrow beam of a torch flitting over the low couch and the bureau set against the far wall. Lissa switched on the light, and Rebecca swung round sharply to face her, shock startling a gasp on her lips, the torch falling with a muffled thud.

'Are you looking for something?' Lissa challenged softly.

Rebecca recovered quickly from the shock of finding that she was not alone. 'You know why I'm here,' she said, her voice rasping in her throat as though she had run a long way. 'You could save us both a lot of trouble by handing over the papers without any fuss.'

Lissa studied her thoughtfully. 'And if I don't care to do that?'

Rebecca's smile was brief and without humour, her lips thinning. 'I can see,' she said, looking around, 'that you use this room as your office. Some of the equipment in here must have cost a small fortune—it would be dreadful, wouldn't it, if there should happen to be an accident?' She picked up a glass paperweight from the desk and tested it in her hand. 'Such fragile things, computers.'

A drift of cool air touched Lissa's bare arms, and she realised that the front door must be open. 'How did you get in here?' she asked. 'Or can I guess? Taking my keys that day was no accident, was it? You used them to get another one cut.'

'I thought it might come in useful,' Rebecca agreed. Her fingers moved slowly over the paperweight.

'Put it down, Rebecca.' Rourke's voice sounded low and even across the silence of the room, and Lissa's heart began to thump wildly against her ribcage. Her gaze ran over him, drinking in the sight of him. He had come, after all. How had he known that she needed him?

His glance met hers for a brief, breathtaking moment, before he started forward, his stride slow, and rangy. Rebecca jerked away from him. Her face was bloodless, etched with inner tension, her fingers gripping the paperweight so that her knuckles were stark and white against the glass.

Rourke stood still. He said quietly, 'Why did you do it, Rebecca? Why did you alter the books? Couldn't you have come to me and told me that you were in debt, that you needed money? I might have made you a loan, or found some other way to help you out.'

'How could I pay back a loan? You don't know what it's like, running a house on just one wage, trying to bring up a child who outgrows everything almost as soon as you've bought it.' Her mouth writhed, her features crumpling as she looked at Lissa. 'Why did you have to come on the scene, meddling? He would never have found out if you hadn't shown up in the office. He trusted me. He never questioned anything I did; nor did Adam.' She shifted the paperweight restlessly in her hands. 'Why did you keep those papers? You ruined everything. It had all been destroyed, all the evidence. . .'

Lissa said bleakly, 'Perhaps I was lying, perhaps there was nothing. . .'

Rebecca stared at her. Slowly, with infinite care, Rourke reached up and untwined the tight band of her fingers from around the heavy ornament. Putting it down on the table, he said flatly, 'There was never any chance; you must know that. Sooner or later we would have discovered what was going on.'

Rebecca shook her head, a wild, remote look clouding her pale blue eyes. Her fingers came up to clutch at his shirt. 'She's a trouble-maker; I knew it from the beginning,' she muttered. 'You know she's working with Blake, making some kind of deal with him. You were angry with her, weren't you? You knew what she was doing; she deserves to have her business fold up around her. She has too much ambition. She should have read the horoscopes and acted on them, then none of this would have happened. She should have gone away when she had the chance. Tell her to go away.'

Lissa watched her, filled with deep sadness. The woman's mind was out of balance, totally disturbed. Even now, she could not accept that it was over, that the deception had to end. She was clinging to the lifeline of Rourke's feelings for her, and who could say that he would deny her that refuge?

'I wish you had come to me, Rebecca,' he said, his voice soft and low. 'I wish you had told me what was wrong, so that I could have helped.' There was such regret, such a bleakness in his eyes that Lissa turned away, her soul crying out in anguish because it was plain for anyone to see how much he cared for this woman who had betrayed him.

'I didn't know what to do,' Rebecca said hoarsely. 'I was so miserable, so desperate. I needed the money. Afterwards, I wanted to tell you, but I was so afraid. I thought you might go to the police, and I didn't know what I would do then.'

'You're overwrought,' he murmured. 'Come and sit down over here.' Rebecca stared at him, but her eyes were wide and unfocused, her mouth working soundlessly. 'Sit down,' he repeated, his tone gentling her as though she were a wounded animal.

She blinked, and did as she was told. 'There's no evidence,' she whispered. 'There's no proof of anything. She said so. She said she was lying.'

'I doubt that's true,' Rourke murmured. 'There will be photocopies, and back-up disks. It's a precaution against losing any work through the computer, you see.'

He looked at Lissa, but he did not need her silent confirmation. He had worked it all out, everything.

Rebecca's face was deathly white, her lips colourless. 'The police,' she said brokenly, 'you called the police. What's going to happen? What am I going to do?'

Rourke knelt down beside her and said softly, 'Forget about the police. I'll deal with them. We'll work it out.'

She began to nod, rocking very gently on the settee. 'You'll send her away, won't you?' she pleaded. 'It's all her fault. It'll be all right again when she's gone.'

'I'll sort it all out,' he said. 'Just sit quietly. You don't have to worry about anything.'

Rebecca subsided, accepting his assurances, and Rourke stood up slowly. He motioned to Lissa and she caught his soundless urging and went with him out of the room. In the small kitchen he said in a low voice, 'Are you OK?'

Lissa breathed deeply. 'Yes. I'm fine.' With him by her side, she could weather any storm.

He touched her face gently, his thumb brushing her cheek, his fingers lightly smoothing back the straying tendrils of her hair. 'You look tired,' he said. 'It's been a long night. It must have been difficult for you.'

'It's over now.' Suddenly, it was not enough that

he was touching her face. She wanted him to hold her properly, to put his arms around her in an embrace that would shut out the world; she needed to feel the hot, demanding pressure of his lips on hers in a kiss that would take away the nagging ache of uncertainty. She wanted it so badly, the longing was a fierce, pulsing desire that surged deep within her.

'Rourke——'

His mouth feathered hers with the softness of thistledown and then, incredibly, as her lips would have clung, he moved away from her, and it was like the sting of rejection, the icy dash of water cascading over her heated flesh.

'I can't stay here,' he said, keeping his voice even. 'I have to do what I can for Rebecca; you know that, don't you? She's been at my side for so many years that it's more than just a business relationship. I must take care of her. She's obviously been under a tremendous strain over the last few months and she needs my help.' His deep blue gaze held hers. 'Can you understand that?'

Shock hit her like a blow. He was doing what Rebecca had asked. He was putting her away from him, because in the end Rebecca was vulnerable, and she meant more to him than anyone else.

Lissa did not know where she found the strength to answer him without betraying anything of her inner turmoil. With an effort, she said distantly, 'I know how much you care. I've always known.' A lump rose in her throat and she felt the sharp sting of tears behind her eyelids. She turned away so that he would not see. Why did love have to settle in all the wrong places? she wondered miserably. Why couldn't she have had just a small taste of the honeyed delight that Rourke's love would have brought, just a fragment of the glowing ember that would have warmed her inside, instead of this cold, bitter emptiness?

'I'll get a doctor over to see her,' Rourke said, a new briskness in his tone. 'There's a clinic, the Marshes, where she could stay, if he thinks that would suit. Where's the phone—in the hall?'

The doctor came within the half-hour, and spent some time with Rebecca before deciding that an ambulance was needed to take her to the Marshes. While they waited, Lissa made hot drinks, then stood apart and listened as Rourke spoke quietly with the woman, who still rocked slowly to and fro on the settee. It was tearing her apart to know how much he must love the pale, blank-eyed girl.

'Why don't you go to bed, Lissa? Try to get some sleep.' His voice cut into her thoughts, and she realised that he had turned to look at her. 'The ambulance has arrived, and you can't do anything more.'

Slowly, like an automaton, she walked to the door, obeying the cool command.

She did not go to bed. Instead, she went and stood by her bedroom window, staring out into the street below, where the lamps cast their pale orange light over the pavement. Perhaps it was shock that made her senses drag in this lethargic way. She had thought herself calm, and in control, but her body felt numb and there was an unreality about everything that was happening.

As she looked down, she saw Rourke helping Rebecca into the ambulance. He climbed in after her, and closed the doors behind them. Lissa pressed her fingertips to the window-pane, as though in some way that would keep him near to her, but the ambulance moved off along the road and the fragile connection was severed.

This was it, then. This was the end. The last she would see of him. The shimmer of tears burned brightly in her eyes, and she rubbed them away with a trembling hand. Tears would not bring him back, but somehow her mind could not register that, and she could not stop the slow salt trickle from creeping down her cheeks.

She went through to the bathroom and ran water into the tub. Her limbs were cold, as though a freezing mixture had seeped into her bones, and she soaked for a while, letting the heat invade her pores. Only when the water began to cool did she at last climb out and towel herself dry. She slid her arms into her silk robe and tied it loosely at the waist.

Walking back into her room, she sat down on the bed and stared unseeingly at the wall. For a long while she stayed there without moving, her mind filled with the dull ache of loss and of longing for what might have been. Then, slowly, she reached for her brush from the dresser, and began to slide it through the unruly tangle of her hair, taming the flyaway curls until they settled into a softly gleaming curtain that fell over her shoulders.

She did not hear the quiet tread on the carpet, and when Rourke came and sat down beside her she drew in a quick, shaky breath, and let the brush clatter to the floor.

'Sorry,' he said. 'I tried not to make a noise, in case you were asleep.' He placed a key on the bedside table. 'I took it from Rebecca in the ambulance,' he explained.

Lissa pulled herself together with an effort. 'I hadn't expected you to come back here tonight. Is everything sorted out for the moment? Is she all right?'

He nodded. 'She's sedated quite heavily, and the doctor will see her again in the morning to get a more thorough picture of things. In the meantime, I've arranged for her daughter to stay with an aunt. I should think Sophie will be OK with her—there's been quite a lot of contact.' There was still that bleak emptiness about his eyes, and Lissa could only guess at the torment he was going through.

She said, her voice remote, not part of herself, 'You must be feeling pretty awful about all this, but I'm sure Rebecca will be well looked after. The clinic you mentioned has a very good reputation.'

He grimaced. 'She'll be safe enough, but I've a feeling it will be a long job to get her back on an even keel. I suppose the divorce must have affected her more than anyone realised.' He pushed a hand through his dark hair. 'I blame myself—I should have noticed what was happening to her.'

'I don't think it was your fault,' Lissa said. 'No one knew, not her relatives, her friends, Adam.' She stared down at her fingers, the silky fall of her hair a refuge to hide behind. 'If anyone's to blame, it's me, for pushing her over the edge. If I hadn't——'

'Don't be silly. You've been under-strain yourself over these last few weeks. You've been threatened and harassed, and worrying about what was around the corner. Who could tell how far she would go? Tonight was just the culmination of what's been building up for a long time.' Rourke's glance shifted over her. 'It's been a bad night for you, hasn't it? You had to wait, knowing that almost certainly she would come here, but without any idea of how dangerous she might be.' He reached out to lift the chestnut curls from her cheek. 'Did you really think I would leave you to face her alone?'

Lissa toyed with the edge of her robe. How had she known what to think?

'Look at me,' Rourke demanded softly, and when she didn't obey his fingers slid around the curve of her throat, his thumb tracing the line of her jaw. He turned her face towards him. 'You did think it,' he said, frowning. 'I came here tonight because I felt that something was wrong, and that you might need me. When you told me about the horoscopes, didn't I tell you I wanted to help? Didn't I tell you I was working on it?' His mouth was firm and hard. 'What kind of man do you think I am, that I could forget something like that?'

She swallowed carefully, her mind skittering back to that day at the office when Rebecca had returned unexpectedly and disturbed them. Faint colour tinged her cheeks at the memories that stirred in her, and she said hoarsely, 'I don't think I understand any of this. You're saying that you came here to help me, but why would you do that? Just lately you've been treating me as though. . .as though you hated me, you've been so angry, so biting. . .' Her eyes darkened. 'Rebecca practically accused me of starting the fire, and you believed her.' She could not control the faint tremor of her mouth, and Rourke's hand lifted, his thumb running gently over the pink fullness of her lips.

'I wanted to see how her mind was working,' he said, but Lissa was not to be appeased. She averted her face from him.

'You were in a rotten mood the whole time. Everything I said, you bit my head off,' she reminded him.

'What did you expect?' he countered, his hands sliding down to grip her shoulders. 'I told you there was no coffee. I found the wretched machine later, in the new extension. That workman has a lot to answer for, I can tell you.'

She did not let his excuse distract her. Nor was she going to give in to the warm and leaping sensations being generated in her by the slow, rhythmic stroking of his fingers. He might well be creating havoc with her pulse-rate, but he was only doing it to comfort her after a bad day; it didn't mean there was anything personal in the action. Anyway, there were other, more important matters that she needed to concentrate on.

'It wasn't just the coffee.' She threw him an emerald glare. 'Only the day before, you came barging into the flat, insinuating that I'd given information to

Richard Blake. How could you believe that I'd do such a thing?'

'I didn't believe it. But I was in a foul temper, and Rebecca hadn't made it any easier by going on about missing papers, and how urgent it was that we had them back.'

'I'll say you were in a temper, and it hadn't changed any when you were back in the office. You were downright nasty to me. You must have known how bad I was feeling, but you didn't care a jot,' Lissa protested.

'Did you care when you walked out on me the day that you told me about the notes and the wine glass, and then Rebecca came back to the office? You went without a backward glance. That was calculated to make me feel really good, wasn't it? You got me all in a lather, and then slid out from under me.'

'So you were feeling frustrated?' Her mouth tightened. 'I'm so sorry; I hadn't realised you had such problems organising your harem.' Stormily, she went on, 'I suppose I was meant to sit back and wait while you danced attendance on your number one girlfriend, was I? "Just wait there, Miss Holbrook, and I'll fit you in when I have a moment." Well, you can think again, because I don't play second fiddle to anyone. It might suit you to dabble around here and there, where you will, but you can count me out.'

He grinned with maddening indifference in the face of her fury. 'Jealous, are you? Good, I'm glad.' His hands clamped her arms. 'Now you know how I felt every time I saw you with Adam, hugging him to you as if you were a bosom friend. I was beginning to hate my own brother-in-law. Lord knows, it was like a fever that threatened to take me over. I needed you so badly and all you ever did to me was cut me down at the knees.'

Her mouth hung open in astonishment. 'I did no such thing.' She frowned darkly. 'And what do you mean, you're glad? Since when were you ever bothered about my feelings? You never spared more than a passing thought for me. You were always too busy putting your arms around Rebecca. I was just a fill-in when she wasn't available.' There was a catch in her voice. 'I know she means a lot to you. It was quite clear tonight how much you care for her, but you'll have to get used to her being away for a month or two. I suppose, as far as you're concerned, love is one thing, sex is another. Well, you'll just have to put your overwhelming sex drive on hold for a while, won't you, because you needn't expect me to cater for your needs.'

His mouth made a tight, grim line, and he began to shake her hard, so hard that her teeth rattled. 'I could turn you over my knee and spank you, you make me so angry,' he said through his teeth. 'What kind of individual would I be, if all I wanted was to replace one woman with another? Don't I get any credit for human decency and normal feelings?' He jerked her again, as if she were a rag doll, eyeing her with disgust. 'I don't know why I bother with you at all. What thanks is this for keeping vigil outside in the street nearly all night? I must have been crazy to think you needed protecting. You could manage perfectly well for yourself, with that whiplash of a tongue.'

'Stop—stop—sh—shaking me,' she managed, when the brunt of his temper had subsided. 'I didn't mean—I mean, I did, but I—I thought you loved her—I thought——Oh, I don't know what to think, I'm so confused,' she finished unhappily.

He shook her again, scowling. 'Of course I don't love her, you stupid woman. I'd never been in love in my life till you came along.' He stared at her furiously. 'Why is it that when I do fall, it has to be for a termagant who drives me out of my head? What kind of life are we going to have together if we're forever at each other's throats?' His lips set in a snarl. 'Something's going to have to be sorted out, do you understand? I'm a gentle soul.' His voice grated on her ears. 'I like peace and quiet.' Glittering blue eyes raked her slender form. 'I like to sit back and let life drift around me. I like the sun setting on a calm sea——' His breath hissed through his teeth. 'I don't like damn great hurricanes descending on me out of nowhere. Have I made myself clear?'

Lissa stared at him, her eyes very wide, very green. She swallowed hard, conscious of his angry face so close to her own, his hands clamping her to him in a vice-like grip. In a very small voice, she said, 'Was that meant to be some kind of proposal? Or did I get that wrong, too?'

'Dammit to hell,' he cursed, letting her go abruptly so that she fell back on the bed in an untidy heap. 'I can't even get that right. What have you done to me?' He glowered at her. 'I had it all worked out what I was going to say, how I was going to make it romantic, and sensual, so that you couldn't possibly turn me down. And now look—I've ruined it. It's all your fault.'

Lissa gazed up at him, at his vexed expression, and tried to quell the smile that pulled at her lips. It was no use. The twitching grew, a bubble of laughter burgeoning inside her, and she began to giggle, trying desperately to hide her mouth with her hand. Her shoulders shook convulsively and she rolled to her side on the bed, curling up.

'Oh, you think it's funny, do you?' Rourke leaned over her, straddling her like a vengeful demon. 'We'll see about that.' Gripping her wrists, he pushed them up on either side of her head, and swooped down to kiss her fiercely, with devastating thoroughness. Beneath the punishing, forceful demand of that kiss, her mouth tingled, then softened, became clinging, eager for the tantalising ministrations of his lips and tongue. She wriggled beneath the powerful surge of his body, conscious of the heat radiating from him, the thunder of his heart beating against her breast. His strong thighs tightened on her, keeping her in place, forcing her to accept his male domination.

'It isn't fair,' she complained breathlessly, when at last they both came up for air. 'You make me feel so strange, so out of control, and all the time you know exactly what you're doing.' Her brows met in a frown. 'Where did you learn how to do that?'

He stared down at her, his eyes glimmering, his body taut over hers. 'I'm working on instinct,' he said thickly, 'but I'm a fast learner, and I've a good enough idea how to keep you in line. I'll subdue you, my little spitfire. I've got you now, and there's no escape.' His mouth curved attractively. 'You think you can have it all your own way, but I know what makes you tick. I know how to turn all your tempestuous heat to sweet purpose.'

Releasing her wrist briefly, he tugged apart the edges of her robe and stared down at her nakedness. She gasped, and tried to cover herself, but he caught her hand and pinioned it once more. 'Beautiful, beautiful Lissa,' he murmured huskily. 'Do you really think you can hide from me? How have I waited so long? You know how much I've wanted you, ached to make you mine.'

His lips slid over her breasts, teasing the rosy peaks to pert arousal, and then moved on to explore the smooth, warm contours of her body, dipping and gliding, fuelling the flames within her until she moved against him restlessly, searching, pleading, making demands of her own.

He released her then, shrugging out of his clothes, and coming back to her, his blue eyes glittering over the satiny perfection of her skin, pink-tinged from the delicate graze of his body on hers. His hands whispered over her, light as silk, seeking out every pale hollow and rounded slope.

Trembling, she ran her fingers over the taut muscles of his chest, and feverishly explored the hard length of him. Her mouth brushed the smooth velvet of his shoulders, and moved down to sweep lightly across his turgid male nipples. He groaned, and shifted a little, tantalising her with the answering flicker of his tongue over the heavy swell of her breast, before he took her mouth again in a long and hungry kiss. With reckless abandon, she pressured herself to him, striving to mould herself to his tough maleness.

His breathing quickened with raw urgency, but he held himself rigid above the provocation of her softly rounded femininity. 'Not so fast,' he whispered huskily, his hands slipping down over her tender curves and kneading gently. 'Not until you agree to all my demands.' His mouth played over the silken plane of her stomach, drifting down over the pliant swelling of her adbomen, and little whimpering cries broke from her lips.

His hands shifted to part her thighs, and allow his fingers to caress the secret, intimate heart of her. His touch was feather-light, circling on her with gratifying recognition of needs she hadn't known existed, coaxing in her sensations that were wild and intensely pleasurable. Her breath caught in her throat as he discovered her moist centre and tenderly probed. It was a new and subtle torment, and she writhed beneath the thrill of his touch, feverishly arching against the eddying bands of tension that enticed her towards some undreamed-of zenith.

'Tell me you love me,' he muttered. 'Let me hear you say it.'

'I love you, I love you,' she said hoarsely. 'Oh, Rourke, please. . .'

'And we'll be married,' he murmured, 'just as soon as it can be arranged.'

'Yes,' she whispered. 'Oh, please, Rourke. . .'

'Is that. . .please we'll be married, or please make love to me?'

'Both,' she cried achingly. 'Can't I have both? I love you, I need you, I want you by my side for all eternity. Can't I have all that?'

He laughed softly. 'Lord, I thought you'd never ask. Sweetheart, you can have whatever you want. Shall we find paradise together?' His voice thickened. 'Come with me, Lissa, let me take you with me.'

He eased into her, and began to move, thrusting, slowly at first, inciting her senses to riot, building up the heat inside her until she thought she must be consumed by the melting rapture of that flame. It was a fusion of body and soul and mind, an exhilaration that soared way beyond anything she had ever known.

The thundering of his heart merged with the beat of her own blood, deafening her to everything around them. Time stood still and suddenly there was only one focus—this mounting, spiralling pressure that set off a high-pitched singing inside her head and made breathing hazardous. He drove her to the very edge of ecstasy and then, as the quivering tide of sensation gathered momentum, he tipped her over and down into the fiery vortex. Ripples of intense pleasure burst around her, and small incoherent cries broke on her lips as joyous release shuddered through her body. Rourke's lips brushed her cheek fleetingly in the instant before his control shattered and he, too, groaned in an explosion of fulfilment.

For a long time afterwards, they lay together,

entwined on the soft covers of the bed, waiting for their breathing to return to normal. At last, Rourke moved, propping himself up on one elbow so that he could gaze down at her.

'I love you, Lissa,' he said huskily. 'I need you to make my life complete. Will you really stay with me for all time, be my wife?'

She hesitated, her eyes clouding a little. 'Can you bear to be held down by the bonds of marriage? I'm afraid I'd make a very jealous lover, Rourke.' Her fingers lifted to stray along the proud angle of his jaw.

A smile tugged at the corners of his mouth. 'Now why do you ask that, I wonder? What was it you threw at me, not so long back? How did you put it? Pisces, and dalliances?' He caught her fingers and kissed them lightly. 'You have no need to be anxious, you know. I haven't wanted to commit myself to anyone until now. There have been women I've liked and respected, but there has been no one I've loved until this moment.' His hands caressed her lightly. 'You are everything I want and need, you fulfil my every fantasy, and I don't want to even think of life without you. They'll be silken bonds, Lissa. I shan't ever let you down.' He bent his head and brushed his mouth gently over hers. 'Will you marry me?' he muttered, his voice thick, and rough.

A soft, shuddery sigh of pleasure hung on her lips. 'I will,' she said huskily, and his arms closed around her, folding her to him.

'Listen,' he murmured, his warm breath drifting

over her cheek. 'Can you hear it? Can you hear the music in your head?'

She nodded. 'What is it?' she whispered, absorbed.

'It's the heavens rejoicing,' he told her with firm surety. 'Didn't you know that Venus holds sway over both of us? It means,' he said, planting a gentle kiss on her soft mouth, 'that our future's secure; that, for all time, you and I will know the pure joy of loving each other.'

STARGAZING

YOUR STAR SIGN: PISCES (February 20th– March 20th)

Pisces is ruled by the planets Jupiter and Neptune, and is the third of the Water signs, which makes you restless, indecisive, intense and sensitive. You are highly imaginative and idealistic, with a tendency to day-dream and to 'switch off' when a difficult situation arises.

Pisceans are kind, charming, sympathetic and true Good Samaritans—but you can sometimes let the needs of others overwhelm you. With your strong need for quiet and privacy, you are very much the home-lover, although your family may exploit your kindness and gullibility by leaving you with all those really nasty tasks around the house!

Your characteristics in love: The most romantic of all the star signs, Pisceans have high expectations of love. You really enjoy the courtship of a new relationship but you tend to idealise your lover and to fall in love with a vision, not real flesh and blood. Unfortunately, although you'll try to turn a blind eye to your lover's inadequacies and transgressions, your illusions are often shattered when reality rears its ugly head.

When you do find your ideal mate, however, you are a caring, intuitive lover, revelling in both the physical and spiritual aspects of the relationship. If you are ever unfaithful it is only in your vivid day-dreams and fantasies!

Signs which are compatible with you: You can find harmony with **Cancer**, **Scorpio**, **Capricorn** and **Taurus**—but enjoy a challenge with **Gemini**, **Virgo** and **Pisces**! Partners born under other signs can be compatible, depending on which planets reside in their Houses of Personality and Romance.

What is your star-career? Pisceans aren't always a walk-over: you can surprise colleagues by being very dominant at work, demanding attention and delegating with confidence. Although not very practical, your interpretive skills and intuitive ability to make money in creative fields make Pisces excel in photography, music, theatre and dance. Alternatively, your unselfish devotion to others and to your work may encourage you to gravitate towards a career in nursing, counselling, religion or education.

Your colours and birthstones: Dreamy Pisceans love the pretty, soothing shades of pale blues, greens and violets.

Your birthstone, the amethyst, is also said to have a calming effect, which makes it ideal for restoring harmony to your sensitive temperament. This purple-red stone is also said to ward off contagious diseases and to prevent the evils of drunkenness!

PISCES ASTRO-FACTFILE

Day of the week: Thursday
Countries: Tonga, Tanzania, Portugal.
Flowers: water lily, white poppy.
Food: Melon, white fish, mushrooms; your idealism makes you choose pure, natural ingredients where possible. Pisceans don't slavishly follow recipes, but allow their creative skills full rein when cooking.
Health: You are prone to bunions, chilblains and other foot problems—and do keep an eye on your alcohol intake and your weight! Highly strung Pisceans might find that massages, or philosophical regimes such as yoga or t'ai chi, will help them relax.

You share your star sign with these famous names:

Elizabeth Taylor   Michael Caine
Liza Minelli   Bruce Willis
Jilly Cooper   Earl of Snowdon
Julie Walters   Paddy Ashdown
Dame Kiri Te Kanawa   Rudolf Nureyev

THE PERFECT GIFT FOR MOTHER'S DAY

Specially selected for you –
four tender and heartwarming
Romances written by popular
authors.

LEGEND OF LOVE -
Melinda Cross

AN IMPERFECT AFFAIR -
Natalie Fox

LOVE IS THE KEY -
Mary Lyons

LOVE LIKE GOLD -
Valerie Parv

Available from February 1993   Price: £6.80

Accept 4 FREE Romances and 2 FREE gifts

Mills & Boon

FROM READER SERVICE

An irresistible invitation from Mills & Boon Reader Service. Please accept our offer of 4 free Romances, a CUDDLY TEDDY and a special MYSTERY GIFT... Then, if you choose, go on to enjoy 6 captivating Romances every month for just £1.70 each, postage and packing free. Plus our FREE Newsletter with author news, competitions and much more.

**Send the coupon below to:
Reader Service, FREEPOST,
PO Box 236, Croydon,
Surrey CR9 9EL.**

- -

NO STAMP REQUIRED

Yes! Please rush me 4 Free Romances and 2 free gifts!

Please also reserve me a Reader Service Subscription. If I decide to subscribe I can look forward to receiving 6 brand new Romances each month for just £10.20, post and packing free.

If I choose not to subscribe I shall write to you within 10 days - I can keep the books and gifts whatever I decide. I may cancel or suspend my subscription at any time. I am over 18 years of age.

Ms/Mrs/Miss/Mr ——————————————— EP30R

Address ———————————————————

—————————————————————————

Postcode ——————— Signature ———————

Next Month's Romances

Each month you can choose from a wide variety of romance with Mills & Boon. Below are the new titles to look out for next month, why not ask either Mills & Boon Reader Service or your Newsagent to reserve you a copy of the titles you want to buy — just tick the titles you would like and either post to Reader Service or take it to any Newsagent and ask them to order your books.

Please save me the following titles:	Please tick	√
BREAKING POINT	Emma Darcy	
SUCH DARK MAGIC	Robyn Donald	
AFTER THE BALL	Catherine George	
TWO-TIMING MAN	Roberta Leigh	
HOST OF RICHES	Elizabeth Power	
MASK OF DECEPTION	Sara Wood	
A SOLITARY HEART	Amanda Carpenter	
AFTER THE FIRE	Kay Gregory	
BITTERSWEET YESTERDAYS	Kate Proctor	
YESTERDAY'S PASSION	Catherine O'Connor	
NIGHT OF THE SCORPION	Rosemary Carter	
NO ESCAPING LOVE	Sharon Kendrick	
OUTBACK LEGACY	Elizabeth Duke	
RANSACKED HEART	Jayne Bauling	
STORMY REUNION	Sandra K. Rhoades	
A POINT OF PRIDE	Liz Fielding	

If you would like to order these books in addition to your regular subscription from Mills & Boon Reader Service please send £1.70 per title to: Mills & Boon Reader Service, P.O. Box 236, Croydon, Surrey, CR9 3RU, quote your Subscriber No:... (If applicable) and complete the name and address details below. Alternatively, these books are available from many local Newsagents including W.H.Smith, J.Menzies, Martins and other paperback stockists from 12th March 1993.

Name:...

Address:...

....Post Code:...........................

To Retailer: If you would like to stock M&B books please contact your regular book/magazine wholesaler for details.

You may be mailed with offers from other reputable companies as a result of this application. If you would rather not take advantage of these opportunities please tick box ☐